MURDER ON THE MENU

THE CANDACE KANE CHRONICLES

JERRI GEORGE

To my mom, who had a voracious appetite for reading, especially mysteries and my cooking! She fell into the grasp of dementia before I could get this project done, but I know she would have loved it. I hope I made you proud, Mom.

Rest in peace, Elaire Alexander Buck 1924-2018

CONTENTS

CHAPTER 1

Bradford Kane drew in a breath of moisture-laden air. Exhausted and sore from a full day navigating the slopes, and a little buzzed from an *après* ski glass of Pinot, the former high school running back surveyed his balcony view. A swathe of indigo painted the skies over the Rocky Mountain peaks as twilight crept over Breckenridge. Clusters of people gathered around an outdoor fire pit below and tiny lights illuminated the open downhill runs.

Waiting for his wife Cynthia to change for dinner, Brad tightened his jaw as thoughts about their afternoon crept in. Their encounter with a mysterious figure outfitted in a granite-gray hoodie and overstuffed ski pants. The man, burdened with photography equipment, navigated his way to Main Street as throngs of skiers exited the packed gondolas like ants to a picnic. While he hastened to focus his telephoto lens, he shoulder-checked Brad and tumbled into Cynthia, knocking her to the ground as they made their way from the lift to their timeshare condo. Brad would have chased down the bastard and smashed his high-tech camera had he not been concerned for his wife, so the guy escaped incident.

"What the hell was that?" she'd asked him, shaken, her soft auburn hair escaped from beneath her crocheted cap.

"That my dear, was probably some paparazzi vying for a shot of Dan. You okay?" he said extending his hand. He and his brother Dan had often been mistaken for each other. Looking up at him, Cynthia's still youthful heart-shaped face and large jade green eyes melted his heart. Brad wasn't the only one who thought she was just as pretty as she had been in high school.

"Well, I don't see it. You're both big men, but aside from the same curly dark hair, I just don't." Cynthia fussed. "It's unreal, this never-ending game of cat and mouse with Dan as the cheese."

"I'm sorry, babe." She was right, of course. The brothers possessed a shock of ebony curls but didn't really resemble each other. Up close, anyone could see Dan's hair was already thinning and salted with a bit of gray. It was amazing what a four-year difference in age made.

She shrugged. "It must be a slow news day. He's probably buying up some land or building a resort around here or something."

Daniel Kane, Brad's only sibling, led a charmed professional life. A millionaire several times over and generous to a fault he was not without an occasional ulterior motive. Dan made their yearly visits to his Rocky Mountain home-base a certainty by buying Cynthia and Brad their own timeshare. It was ideal for keeping his brother's family close without a collection of juvenile trappings intruding on his own bachelor existence.

Brad had politely rejected the initial offer but acquiesced once a break from the pressures of work came secondary to entertaining and keeping pace with their rambunctious teenage daughter, Candace, who barely contained herself every time friends accompanied her to their winter wonderland. If it meant tolerating those publicity hounds who stalked his brother and by extension, Brad and his family, then so be it.

"Do you think we're getting old, Cyn?" Brad asked as he

busied himself collecting their ski equipment scattered in the snow. "I mean look at us, huffing and puffing from the lift to the lodge and now getting run over by some camera jockey?" He grimaced playfully and fell to his knees after slinging the gear over his shoulder, acting overcome in a conspicuous effort to make light of her spill.

"I won't admit it if you don't." She slapped him on the rear with her gloved hand and scrambled to her feet. "Come on, I'll race you. First one in the hot tub wins!" she shouted over her shoulder.

"Wins what?" He countered, but she was well ahead and out of ear shot, sashaying her perfect size eight frame up the embankment. Dressed smartly in a Gorsuch ski outfit and Olympic regulation boots, he had to admit that his wife's natural taste for high-end clothing was trumped only by their ability to purchase it wholesale as owners of Kane Manufacturing of Miami.

Her playfulness amused Brad. Cynthia was a nut and knew how to turn him on after almost twenty years. She kept him young. He was glad he wasn't single like Dan. He could never live like him. However, it would be nice to have a ski caddie or valet to carry all his junk up the hill like his brother likely did.

Turning his attention to the appearance of Cynthia who, bundled from head to toe in cream color fur, was delighted by the idea of the horse-drawn sleigh ride and fondue supper he had booked. It was, after all, the perfect romantic gesture, reminiscent of their honeymoon ride in Vermont when Brad's breath froze like a handlebar mustache atop his lips. Tonight, the Lederhosen-dressed driver cut the sleigh of twenty passengers through pristine fresh powder. They rode for miles, bundled in heavy coats, snuggling beneath handmade down quilts, the whisper-quiet broken only by the sound of bells jingling from the horses' leather straps. Passengers were encouraged to sing traditional holiday songs, and Brad chimed in with his best impression of

Bing Crosby as the jovial voices filled the snow-packed wilderness.

The lodge's rooftops peaked above drifts of white, resembling a gingerbread house buried in whipped icing. The couple was greeted heartily by a costumed toy soldier who seated them at a cozy table near frost-covered windows in front of a roaring fire. Their faces thawed over simmering pots of pungent cheese and wine. Pieces of crusty French bread and assorted fresh vegetables were plunged into the gooey concoction, followed by bananas, strawberries and marshmallows dipped into dark melted chocolate.

They toasted the night and the end of their vacation and agreed their entire trip had been equally as delicious but couldn't help remarking how much their daughter Candace would have enjoyed it. Passionate about cooking and documenting the differences in local eateries, her leather-bound diary contained ideas and techniques from chefs she had interviewed while on the road.

While Brad mustered the strength for one final visit to the lodge Jacuzzi, Cynthia packed up their condo. Lucky for him his partner in both life and business had taken a more conservative approach to the day, executing fewer downhill runs and taking only sips of wine at dinner. Cynthia was the wiser choice to navigate the SUV back down the mountainside into Denver. The decision was an easy one since Brad knew she preferred driving anyway and was a woman who liked being in control of her own destiny.

He was grateful Dan had thought of every last detail when arranging their getaway, from the lift tickets to breakfast room service and transportation to and from the airport. It didn't take long before Dan's borrowed Chevy Tahoe was fully packed and headed down a quiet mountain road from the ski resort to civilization with Cynthia at the wheel.

On this particular January evening, the sky was dark and

sprinkled with stars, like thousands of crystals atop a holiday sugar cookie. Billowy cotton-candy clouds blanketed the mountaintops and threatened snow.

"Are you sure you're okay to make it down the mountain, honey? We could change our reservation and stay the night." Brad offered but knew better. She'd never delay getting home to Candace. Out of sight but never out of mind. That girl—all of thirteen going on thirty—was a living, breathing appendage of his wife and their very reason for living. "Yes, I'm fine. I'd prefer taking a nap in the airport than chancing getting snowed in up here. I can't wait to see Candace," she said. "I know dear. I think she'll flip over the necklace we bought." He patted the14-karat gold-etched aspen leaf tucked securely into his jacket pocket.

She said, "Do you think we can get her to come with us next year? She'll be old enough to ski without a chaperone."

She'll also be old enough to avoid going anywhere with her parents, Brad thought pragmatically. Candace was mature about many things but still needed protection from a life of privilege and indulgence in his opinion. He and his wife had set the stage but it was his brother who embellished and fine-tuned life's experiences. Despite it all, their little girl was growing into an accomplished young woman, and although her grades were average, she played piano, acted in her drama club, and volunteered with Habitat for Humanity in hurricane-ravaged South Florida.

～

Cynthia noticed the recently plowed road. A skim of ice still coated it. A quick glance into the rearview mirror revealed a solitary set of car headlights between two snowbanks.

Two dots, so tiny, looked like stars suspended in the sky dancing behind them. Cynthia peered down at the speedometer confirming she was indeed obeying the speed limit then looked at the reflection again; the specks had now become splashes of white piercing through the night as flurries began to fall around them. She switched on the windshield wipers, setting them to react intermittently. The natural curve of the road tightened around the mountainside and the lights behind them disappeared.

Brad was already asleep. His head was supported by a pillow which squished his face against the passenger window. Cynthia smiled. He needed a haircut. Perhaps then he wouldn't be so easily mistaken for his brother.

It had been an interesting seventeen years of marriage. The two had met and started dating in high school when the Kane brothers moved to Florida from Massachusetts after their father's death. At first, she felt funny choosing one brother over the other since they both chased almost anyone in a skirt and competed over everything. But there was something about Brad's big blue eyes and teddy bear demeanor that won her over. It didn't hurt that he seemed to be the underdog in his sibling rivalry with his older brother. Even though Brad was smarter, Dan had a larger than life, magnetic personality—a little too much so for a shy, freckled redhead like her.

They had married just after graduation. Brad put his business-head and some inheritance money behind Cynthia's natural talent for clothing design, and their label soon grabbed national attention as Miami Beach sportswear outfitters. Traveling from coast to coast frequently, Cynthia was taken by surprise when Candace came along. Juggling a family and a busy career was challenging, but they managed. Money had a way of smoothing over the rough spots, and she was certain Brad was in it for the long haul.

Snowflakes began falling at a steady rate. What a beautiful sight. To think, she'd be squinting against the powerful Florida sun in just a few hours, not peering through a night streaked with white. She checked herself in the mirror. As her freckles looked back at her, she spotted the car behind them once again traveling at an impressive clip. Cynthia sped up to widen the gap, giving the driver more space coming into the next bend. Perhaps they were faced with an emergency and needed to pass.

Craning to see over her left shoulder out the side window, Cynthia tried to catch a glimpse around the mountain edge then corrected her gaze back to the rearview mirror. Her heart quickened. Larger and more prominent, the headlights suddenly appeared directly behind her but unexpectedly vanished under the truck's oversized rear tinted window.

"Now that's odd," she said aloud. Her husband appeared dead to the world, snoring. She considered waking him, but he roused on his own, sensing a change in her driving.

"What's up babe?" Brad stretched his arms up over his head and shifted, trying to find a more comfortable position.

"Oh nothing, I guess. A car behind us acting weird. At first I thought it was a cop."

"What? Where?" He looked behind them. "Were you speeding or something?"

"No! Of course not," she answered. "You're the one that speeds." She had actually started to purposefully slow down. She leaned forward. It was hard to see through the snowy mess left behind by the wipers.

While rubbing his eyes he asked, "Was I out long?"

"Not very." Cynthia's brow furrowed as she suddenly caught sight of the lights again. The other car slid back, revealing itself after practically kissing her rear bumper. They hadn't tried to pass. She braked, trying to distinguish the make or model of the car in the glow of her taillights but was unable to see anything except the shape of a modern mid-size sedan, and beyond it, a shower of rapidly falling snow against a backdrop of black.

"What time is it?" Brad was regaining clarity.

"Around ten," she said. "I think I should slow down and force this joker behind us to pass. He's going pretty fast and keeps riding my bumper."

He released his seat belt, twisting to obtain a better look. "I thought…"

WHAM! A sudden and powerful impact propelled their vehicle forward with the force of a gunshot. Cynthia's foot popped off the brake like a recoiled spring. If she hadn't had the presence of mind to brace her arms, she might have smashed her face into the steering wheel.

Brad was thrown forward. The side of his head slammed into the dashboard, crumpling his cheekbone. "What the hell…?" he mumbled with blood streaming from his nose.

"Are you okay? That stupid fool hit us!" Cynthia called out. The driver had purposefully plowed into their rear bumper. Why would anyone do that?

Their car coasted from the force of the hit. Oddly, the attacking car was close behind. Thank God Brad he was conscious. Cynthia struggled to regain control on the ice.

Blood was streaming from under his brow "You need…to find…a place to pull over."

"I know. We need to call the cops and an ambulance." She vowed to give that lunatic a piece of her mind. Cynthia's eyes scoured the roadside for a place to stop, but only icicles dangling from rocky crevices were present in the moonlight.

The sedan followed slowly, not quite as close as before, weaving as if anxious to pass. Was the driver hoping to get away or simply reassess his prey like a wild animal stalks before springing? Cynthia sped up to reach a wider place in the road. Her palms were sweating beneath her gloves.

"What are you doing?" Brad fumbled to reconnect his seatbelt.

"I'm trying to get out of his way. He's on our tail, and there's so much ice on the edges of the road." The lane straightened ahead. Recognizing her opportunity, Cynthia crossed over the yellow center line, caring little for the legalities as much as getting them out of harm's way. At least the road here was passable except for the sheer wall of rock on the right.

The other driver also crossed and sped up, advancing with renewed fervor. Cynthia hit the accelerator to catapult them forward. The assailant, obviously hell bent on plowing right through them, closed in, looming again at a dangerous clip.

"Oh...my...God!" Cynthia shouted with an emphasis on each word. "Brad!"

The deafening sound of crushing metal and the steel-on-steel collision interrupted him from answering, jolting them both. The rearview mirror wrenched free from the windshield, bounced against the dashboard, and caught Cynthia above her right eye as it came to rest on the back seat. The unbridled force of the impact twisted her back and shoulders. She had no idea if she was badly hurt and had no time to waste. The SUV slid, fishtailing on black ice. By now, the back of it would certainly be crumpled like an overplayed accordion.

"Pull off, Cyn, pull OFF!" Brad yelled, attempting to grab the wheel.

"I'm trying." She regained control, but the road was diminishing again.

Towering cliff formations left little margin for error. Their attacker followed, ramming their vehicle one more time, sending it careening out of control toward the opposite edge of the summit; their bodies thrown with centrifugal force to the right.

"Brad?" He was slumped over, senseless, as if beaten and battered in a fist fight.

Cynthia began to sob. *"God, please help us."* She thought about Candace. She wanted to hold her.

Tightening up on the wheel and slamming on the brakes, she decided to end this chase once and for all, but the other driver at a near crawl, revved his engine and collided once again with their bumper. This time their wheels skated and abruptly left the embankment. Their car caught air along with everything not bolted down–her purse, their map, coffee cups, and camera–as if they were astronauts in orbit.

A snow-laden, tree-filled landscape reflected in their high beams with only an abyss below. It seemed the SUV forever was airborne, but time didn't tick by on the digital dashboard clock. A distinct whoosh from the free-spinning tires could be heard, otherwise there was nothing but an eerie absence of sound, a hush suspended over the dark valley below as the void prepared to accept them.

It felt like skiing. The familiar downhill rush, exhilarating yet frightening. Pine limbs, blanketed by snow, snapped as they passed. Fresh powder piled high surrounded them while village lights twinkled below. The tires found temporary footing, catching each mogul and landing hard, causing her head to hit the roof and in rapid succession. She gnashed her teeth together. Dazed and out of focus in a surreal state of mind, Cynthia came to a realization that the trees, snow, empty abyss, mangled metal, and their bodies would soon become one.

The sheer bulk of the SUV had caused them to pick up speed as it tumbled down the mountainside, end over end, then side over side, barreling out of control. Her stomach pitching at a rollercoaster clip, Cynthia raised her hands to wipe her tears only to find them mixed with blood and a bone protruding from her right wrist. In that split second, she yearned for unconsciousness as she reached for Brad. *Not us, not now. Why?*

With her daughter present in her mind's eye, her thoughts filled with a mother's angst. The bottom of the mountain materialized. The crash was significant and final. The stillness of a dark winter night once again enveloped the valley.

CHAPTER 2

D an Kane walked slowly into the kitchen of his fashionable Key West townhome elevated above the tropical waters. His muscular arms slung across his chest, hands clasping elbows, almost hugging his large frame. Broad across his shoulders and neck, and narrow in the hips, many people saw him as an imposing figure. It was his mannerisms that softened this demeanor. The way he paused and drew in a breath between phrases, his clever wit and propitious winks worked well on the ladies. At this moment though, no charm was exhibited, only concern darkened his steely blue eyes.

"Jesse, my brother and sister-in-law are missing."

"What? *Dios Mio!*" As was her habit, his chef, housekeeper, and confidant for many years had just put the finishing touches on the dinner dishes and set the automatic coffee pot. The retro 50's tile countertops and stainless-steel appliances gleamed. The louvered blinds were drawn, obstructing the view of the Gulf of Mexico from the window, but the setting sun shone brightly enough to seep in around the edges and reveal the concern on her face.

"The police station in Breckenridge got a call from their factory here in Miami. No one has seen or heard from them since the night before last. They were supposed to return to work today but never made it in." He drew in a breath, and his shoulders heaved. He sat down at the cold metal kitchen table. Although it was decorated in bright yellow with touches of red, the room seemed dim.

"They told me there's been no sign of them since Saturday night. According to security, they skied the whole day and left after dinner. The airline shows they had reservations to fly out of Denver into Miami on a red-eye, but there's no indication of them cancelling and no record of them on the plane. The most puzzling part is they haven't made contact with Candace."

"Oh no, Mr. Dan! I canno' believe that they would not call her unless something was terribly wrong," she spoke in fractured English, rolling her 'r's. A frown crinkled her tan and weathered face which suddenly looked older than her forty-two years. Her generous physique seemed to shrink within the folds of her chef's jacket as she collapsed into a chair. He watched as she pressed her palm flat to her chest and grasped the small ornate cross she wore around her neck.

"Exactly. That's my concern. Brad and I lost our father when we were just kids. If something's happened to them, I don't know what Candace will do." He reached across the kitchen table to place a hand reassuringly on hers. The kitchen fell silent. A tear trickled down Jesse's cheek.

Dan had hired Jessica Alvarez when she was employed as the head chef at a popular Mexican restaurant in Denver. A regular customer, Dan was so seduced by her cooking that he stood up one house-packed Saturday night broadcasting his intentions. With a belly full of her pork tamales and a few too many margaritas, he asked them to raise their glasses and join him in a toast to *his* new executive chef. Dan Kane knew what he wanted and had the money to make it happen.

"Do you want my help to pack a bag, *señor?*" A term she used more in endearment than in title. "Will you go to Denver now or in the morning?" She slowly rose, the metal legs of the red vinyl chair scuffed across the black and white checkered tile floor. Characteristically adjusting the waist of her houndstooth pants, and smoothing her coffee colored hair with both palms to make certain it was still in a severe bun, she took a tissue from her pocket and wiped both eyes.

"No, not Colorado...not just yet, the police are combing the area in search of their car and anyone who may have seen them recently. But I think I should send for Candace. If they don't come up with something, or when they do, she should be here with me, with us." He searched her face.

"*Sí*, yes, *muy bueno*. I think she will like that. She can cook with me, we can shop and go to the beach, and if..." She stopped.

"That's what I was thinking," he said, picking up where she left off and locking in on her gaze. He didn't want to acknowledge what he guessed was her next thought. "I know we have the investor's barbeque tomorrow night, and it's a lot of work, but if you don't mind having her around, I think I'll send my car for Candace tonight."

Without waiting for Jesse's answer, one she didn't need to give, he pulled a small piece of paper from his pocket and focused on the scrawled words. "I guess she's staying with friends near their house in Miami Shores." Drawing another deep breath, he quietly added, "Jesse, I'm glad you're here." He rose, hugged her around the shoulders and strode off toward the study.

Dan's study was actually one of four bedrooms in a two-story townhouse supported by stilts off the southwest Florida coast. A vacation home for entertaining clients, it offered a breathtaking view of the gulf. The investment banker had always been drawn to water. Raised near the ocean in a small coastal Massachusetts town, he and his younger brother spent memorable days on the beaches of Cape Cod. After their father died, the boys moved with their mother to a different shore—south Florida. The brochures had described it "where the sand is silky and the waters are warm as a bathtub year 'round."

This home and his Breckenridge condo were two favorites for spending what little time he had with family, most of it commandeered by skiing--—either down a mountain or behind a speedboat.

His hand shook as he made the call. He had no idea what to say to Candace. An adept communicator on many fronts, he found dealing with young people a challenge. Candace, or CJ, as he often called her, had become the exception to the rule. She had wormed her way into his heart from the moment she was born.

He would do anything for her. But, what if the unimaginable loomed ahead...?

CHAPTER 3

C andace soon discovered her parent's will gave her uncle Dan full custody and guardianship until she turned 21. She moved from her home in Miami Shores, and all of her personal stuff was stored while she stayed with Uncle Dan in the Keys until he sent her away to school. She thought it was bad enough to go to a brand-new school and be forced to make new friends, but sending her to an all-girls boarding school was just mean.

"My mom would never have done this to me," she insisted, standing on the deck of her uncle's townhouse, arms crossed in front of her locked in anger, the only feeling she was able to express. She studied the ocean searching for some comfort in the expanse of water.

Dan pleaded his case. "I know you need time, CJ, and I want to do right by you, but my life has no room for a young girl full time."

The police report and the insurance policies used words "common calamity" to explain what had put them in this situation, but for her it meant more than losing both parents. She was losing everything. What did he know anyhow? He only had one sibling growing up and he was a boy. She had overheard him tell his attorney in secret that he wasn't prepared for hormones, tears and growing breasts. Really? It was no picnic for Candace either. An only child had a closer, more intense relationship with her parents. She was Daddy's little girl and could throw a ball dead center and wrestle without crying. As Mom's best friend, there was clothes shopping, painted fingernails and sweet smelling everything. Cooking and baking, even when trying to diet, entertaining and smiling, even with menstrual cramps, and swimming in the hot Florida sun with skin that boiled like live lobster. Today she felt like tossing a ball around with her dad, and she wanted to talk to her mom. Especially about what Uncle was proposing. This was the first time she had to negotiate without advice, make a deal with him and show him her Kane business skills.

"Look at this place." He waved his arm broadly. "It's a tropical bachelor pad on stilts, sitting atop the Gulf of Mexico with a fully stocked bar. This place is no place for a teenage girl to grow up."

"But, Uncle, I won't be any trouble. I can move in with one of my friends from school—and go back to *my* school. I can see you on breaks. Please don't make me move away." Candace was distraught. "I can't believe you're sending me to a boarding school!"

"Candace, your dad and mom entrusted me with a great responsibility. Now don't get me wrong, I'm honored with the task of raising you in their stead, but I've never been a parent, never even been married, and I don't know anything about raising a young lady."

Her voice was almost shrill. A look of abject torture crossed her face. "But I won't know anyone. I already lost Mom and Dad. Now you want me to lose everyone else?"

"CJ, I'm afraid you're going to need to adjust to a move one way or the other. I can't live in Miami Shores. I don't have that kind of life. I travel all the time," he said.

"I know, but I *love* my school! Why did this have to happen?"

She stomped one foot and turned her head briskly away from her uncle to hide the tears rolling down her cheeks. Candace stared out at the expanse of clear aqua-colored water searching for a lifeboat, but only hungry pelicans were on the edge of the dock, looking for discarded scraps that collected against the pilings.

"I don't know the answer to that question, honey. But I know I can't very well drag you all over the world or have a tutor in every city. It would make your life so tough. Your parents' wish, if anything were ever to happen to them, was for you to complete school in a very secure, stable environment. I don't know why they chose me, God knows, but your life isn't a poker game." He touched her arm pulling her to him and tried to catch her eye.

She felt like he was reeling in a prized catch; she gulped air in desperation like a dying fish through gills.

"I'll tell you what, let's compromise," he finally said. "You go to this private school, which came highly recommended by the way, 'til the end of the year. Give me time to find a suitable place for us to live while you finish. Maybe I can see what settling down on the ranch looks like, and in the meantime, if you find you like it at the school you can stay. If you hate it like you think you will, you need only to endure one more move, but we will settle down somewhere...deal?"

"You mean it?" She sniffled and looked up with heavy tear-soaked lashes—the same long lashes her mom had possessed. "Together? Just the two of us?"

"Well, us and Jesse...you don't want us to starve, do you?" He gave her a big warm toothy smile that was so much like her dad's. He even had the same small gap between his front teeth, the one she had hoped to get braces for someday. It would forever remind her of her father.

CHAPTER 4

The racket of pots clanging, dishes being scraped and stacked, and the mere hustle and bustle in the kitchen, made it hard for Candace to hear her cell phone ring. Luckily, she felt it vibrate in her apron pocket. Pulling it out quickly, she looked at its screen and read the number display. It was the landline at the ranch. Uncle Dan wouldn't be calling at this hour if it wasn't really important. Since the day her parents died nearly 15 years ago, he rarely let one go by without touching base. But so late?

"Hello..." Candace could barely hear over the din and stepped onto the terrace. There was static on the other end of the line, no doubt caused by a lack of signal at the mountain lake house where the reception was taking place. It had been three years since she'd started her catering business after working professionally for some top Denver companies, culinary school and time in France. She never tired of working venues with statuesque peaks as their backdrop. Rows of trees climbed the mountainside like armies of candlesticks. In the winter they were laden with snow, but in the summertime every needle on each branch could be seen in the moonlight like fanned peacock feathers. A fragrant cloak of pine and birch filled the night air.

"Hello?" Uncle Dan's normally booming voice was a breathless whisper. "I need you to come down to the ranch now, tonight... I..."

The line disconnected.

"Uncle Dan? Uncle DAN?" she said louder the second time.

CJ wiped her hands on her apron as she cradled the phone between her cheek and shoulder and then allowed it to slide down the sleeve of her crisp white coat. Catching it, she pushed redial. The call linked straight to voicemail. CJ gingerly inserted her body through the French doors at the opposite end of the patio and scanned the ballroom for Anton while trying to remain inconspicuous. Surrounded by pine walls and floors and panoramic windows that framed the lake beyond, it was a place where brides could add their own touches. That evening the room was draped in cream-colored lace with touches of roses and baby's breath.

Candace and her Russian partner, Anton Yermilov, were a popular Denver catering duo who often worked in mountain locations late into the night. Focused on breaking down the evening's buffet in preparation for the bride and groom to make their exit, Anton was instructing servers from least thirty feet away. She pushed the button to send her call again and it went straight to voicemail. What was Uncle Dan trying to tell her? Was she disconnected from his end or was it the poor signal here? She had to get him back on the line.

I need to tell him where I am and that I can't possibly get to the ranch for at least four hours, even if I leave right away. She ran her dainty but calloused fingers through her hair, tousling her bangs and frowned, turning her otherwise smooth complexion into a forehead full of tiny wrinkles. CJ bit her lower lip in thought and drew a tentative breath. She ducked back onto the patio away from the eighty or so guests that remained.

Her uncle's ranch was just outside Gallegos, New Mexico. He would know better than anyone that taking a plane would serve no purpose. Even if she could get a private one at this hour, there would be no car at the other end and no transportation services operated within miles of the closest airport.

Anton came up stealthily behind her, pulled her to him, cradled her in his arms and whispered, "Come, let me steal you away from this place, my lovely кукла." Nuzzling her neck, his teeth pulled at a spray of her reddish blonde hair. He tugged at the hand which still clutched her phone and twirled her around as if dancing. "It is time for our escape, ha ha!" He flashed a grin and made a grand sweeping gesture with his other arm like Prince Charming leading the way.

Nearly twenty-five, lean and tall with a body that could rival Baryshnikov in his heyday, Anton was wiry and quick on his feet. Like many young Russian men, he possessed an angular jaw and high cheekbones. His cropped chestnut brown hair and expressive ice blue eyes proved a handsome combination, and it was easy to see why women were attracted to him. Even Candace was not immune. At six-foot-five he towered over the kitchen staff which made taking command easy, and take command he did.

One good thing about Anton as she had told her uncle after their first job together was his apparent obliviousness to his God-given magnetism. When he worked, he was focused and intent on the fine art of preparation. Every minute detail was to be precisely carried out or heads would roll, but when he relaxed, he had an easy-going manner and an unexpected bawdy sense of humor that showed up routinely.

"Anton!" With her voice at an uneasy pitch, she reeled around stopping him mid-gesture. "Uncle just called, I don't know why, but he...he sounded upset, out of breath. He asked me to come to the ranch right away, and then we were cut off!" She was worried.

Anton's accent charmed each syllable as it left his lips. He focused on her intently. "CJ, calm down. Tell me, what did he say, exactly?"

She drew in a breath and let it out slowly. Her small frame was dwarfed beneath even the smallest chef's jacket typically cut for a man's physique. "I don't know exactly, he said he needed me to come. He was whispering, and it was so noisy with the DJ. The phone had a terrible connection. I think it's from being up here in the mountains. Anyway, after just a few words...it went dead. I've tried to get him back three times, but it goes straight to voicemail. Anton, he's never called this late, you know that."

"I do know that he would not want you to worry so much. I am sure he is probably fine. He maybe wanted you to call him back...after." His voice was calm and even, although the circumstances were unusual.

"After? After what?" she responded impatiently. "I just think something is really wrong."

"Look, your uncle knows you are with me, and we are at work, no?" His hands held her arms firmly, close to her body. He shook her gently. "You know how he hates to interrupt. He's always so careful about making sure we concentrate on business, even more so now he's retired...yes?"

He was peering directly into her eyes. She sighed. He always seemed to ground her. Why she never gave into his flirting boggled her mind sometimes. Life seemed more simple keeping things purely business, but at this moment, she really wanted him to reassure her and hold her together.

She looked at him pleadingly. "I know, but..."

"He probably stayed up late, thinking of something he wanted to tell you. Maybe he heard the party in the background and just hung up. Don't jump to, how you say...conclusions?"

"But you didn't hear his voice. Will you call him again for me on your phone? And I'll try to reach Jesse. I liked it better when the staff was around and kept an eye on things. Just because he's retired it doesn't mean he can do everything on his own! You men. You all think you're so indestructible!"

Anton smiled as he dialed the phone, dimples forming on his cheeks. He shook his head and shrugged. Candace knew she was not the first headstrong female Anton had dealt with in his life. On the contrary. Anton was raised by his mother and grandmother who were both strong-willed and hot-tempered women.

As the catering staff loaded the truck ready to close down the venue, it was nearly eleven. Anton pushed CJ. into leaving early since neither of them could reach Dan, and the only way to satisfy both their curiosity and concern was for her to go to the ranch.

"I'll handle everything here. You go and drive with care," he said. Anton had been her counterpart and right arm for the past three years. He was blessed with a natural talent for working with food and an ability to create and experiment with the zeal and finesse of a much older and experienced culinary master. He surrendered to his passion, giving up his mother's idea of architectural college, and trained with Candace at Johnson and Wales, a choice his mother still cursed in letters from the old country.

As Candace navigated out of the Front Range alone heading south on I-25 out of Colorado, she thought about nothing but Uncle Dan, the man who had rescued her fifteen years before.

Nearing the border between Colorado and New Mexico, Candace decided to call her best friend. Dawn was one of the few people who could understand what she was feeling at the moment, but there was no answer. She left a message with as many details as she could proffer, which was hardly anything.

The pair had grown up together. As toddlers they were transported from one worldwide locale to another, napping while their mother's sun-bathed and their driven fathers, or in Candace's case, father and uncle, created new ways to bring in cash. As they grew into prepubescence, even their nannies had difficulty reigning them in.

Fair skinned, fine food-loving Candace, became a plump, curly haired strawberry blonde, with freckles and a fetching smile who found comfort in ordering room service, peeking into dining rooms and shadowing hotel staff with primped buffets for dinner. Dawn, a year older and prematurely boy crazy, was a foot taller than Candace ever since childhood, sported sleek shoulder-length chestnut colored hair, and eyes the color of chocolate M&M's. Left to her own devices, Dawn gravitated toward hotel room mini-bars, and poolside cabanas strutting her developing bikini-clad body.

After Candace had been sent to boarding school, they reconnected in the summers, sharing lessons in tennis and golf from pros in the Hamptons. A peculiar pair, the likes of salt and pepper or Laurel and Hardy, were very different but had found a connection in an odd and lonely world.

Before reaching the highway to Gallegos, Candace placed another call that elicited no response.

"Now would be a good time for you to use that sixth sense of yours and call me, Jesse," she said aloud. Her hands gripped the leather steering wheel cover with worry. She had never considered anything bad happening to Uncle Dan.

CHAPTER 5

B y the time Candace reached the ranch, she could tell something was definitely awry. Her uncle insisted she come tonight, but the house and courtyard fountain were dark, and the only movement were shadows of tree limbs reflecting in the moonlight, eerily dancing like puppet figures on the barrel tiled roof. In the late-night darkness, she barely saw beyond the house's wood frame that held the pine logs of the structure securely in place.

Dan and his foreman Nate had painstakingly hammered and glued each one of those logs closely together when Candace was no more than eight. They erected the entire six-bedroom, four-bath, one-level home during one of the summers Candace and Dawn stayed on the ranch. The girls climbed the surrounding trees and swam in the five-acre lake as the smell of freshly hewed wood permeated the air with the echo of hammers striking heavy nails resounded in their heads. Those scents and sounds were just as much a part of Candace's memories as the soft feel of the bare hollow boards giving way underfoot tonight.

The unlatched door, made of heavy wooden planks resembling an old storm-weathered ship, was ajar. It was unlikely it simply blew open. Decorated with a wrought-iron levered handle, large Spanish style hinges, and a black metal grate which covered a beveled window at its center, Candace pushed the ornate door open. Something she didn't have the strength for until the age of ten.

"Uncle Dan?" she called, raising her voice only slightly. The night was so still. "Uncle?"

Her fingers touched the handle. She pushed, and the door gave ever so slightly. Swollen from the chilly night, it creaked. Candace wished she'd left the headlights on to her SUV so it could have shined into where she stood. It was pitch black inside. She leaned into the doorway and peered through the darkness.

"Uncle Dan, where are you? I got here as soon as I could." Her concern showed in her voice. It was oddly vacant and lonely feeling with the ranch hands and Jesse not there. Her hand groped the wall for the light switch. Her reach successful, the room was suddenly ablaze from the overhead deer-antler chandeliers. She saw the familiar dark brown dual-leather sofas draped in Aztec-patterned saddle blankets. Wooden rockers with upholstered ottomans and Uncle Dan's plaid overstuffed chair filled the rest of the room. Built-in oak shelves displayed Dan's library of favorite books and collectible statues of deer, elk and bear in a variety of sizes and mediums. Leftover wall space provided a home to animal-head trophies. Three elk, two antelope and his prized safari-slain rhinoceros hung proudly center stage over an enormous stone fireplace. Several bright, intricately woven Indian rugs scattered the floor, the largest one under the mammoth dining room table capable of seating sixteen.

"Uncle Dan!" Candace screamed when she discovered his body crumpled on the floor. She was unprepared seeing his massive form sprawled across the threshold of the fireplace.

She ran to his side and fell to her knees. With trembling fingers, her hand tentatively touched his wet matted hair. A trickle of blood had puddled on the floor. "Oh, Uncle, can you hear me?"

There was no movement, but Candace could hear him breathing slightly with her ear gently placed on his chest. Her limited medical knowledge left her at a loss. She didn't know where to touch him or what to do. She could easily assess the condition of a piece of meat roasting in an oven, but that training was no help here.

Grabbing her cell phone, half talking to herself and half expressing her plight to the room at large, she pondered aloud, "I can't get you up or get you into the car all by myself. What can I do to help you?"

She dialed 911.

Candace took his hand and held it, fingers entwined, like she did when she was young, rocking back and forth on her heels in worry as she waited for the ambulance. The hospital was in town. Almost an hour from the ranch by choice. In fact, it would be farther if it wasn't for poorly accessible water and electrical connections in this part of New Mexico. Uncle Dan always liked Gallegos but it was years behind in population, planning, zoning and utilities. An hour seemed like an interminable amount of time to wait for a speeding ambulance.

Candace jumped up and dashed to the kitchen, grabbing a dish towel and soaking it under cold running water. They had dug their own well. She remembered her uncle hands-on with the kitchen, too. The walls were covered with numerous substantial oak cabinets with wrought-iron pulls. The black and gold granite countertops he had installed were quite forward-thinking at the time along with the deep porcelain farm sink and stainless-steel worktables. It was nothing but the best for the Kane family patriarch.

Her mind flashed back to countless parties and celebrations they had on school holidays and summer breaks. Guests loved to hang out while pots of spicy beans and creamy sauces were simmered, and pitchers of margaritas flowed, served up in over-sized decorative stemware. Times after she, Jesse and Uncle became a family. She shuddered looking at the kitchen now. Dark, quiet, empty, the way it would be without Uncle Dan.

She wrung out the cloth and returned to Dan's side, dabbing it across his brow then placed it on his forehead. *Shock*, she thought to herself. He might be suffering from shock. A solution quickly came to mind, and she grabbed one of the fur pelts thrown across the arm of the sofa. She wrapped it around him, leaned over his nearly lifeless body and kissed his cheek.

Candace began to pray, then to ponder. How did this happen? A tall lamp had been pulled off a nearby end table and a fireplace poker lay next to him. Had he grabbed it to defend himself against an intruder, or did he simply have a heart attack or stroke and collapse while tending the fire and hit his head? God forbid a thousand times.

"I knew you shouldn't have stayed out here all by yourself! You're going to be alright now. I'm here." Her soothing conversa-tion with the room continued as she rocked back on her feet again. A chill ran through her body. Deserts were oddly cold at night, but the wood in the fireplace was new and void of any sign of flame or ash. There was certainly no reason for her uncle to need a poker. Weathered cardboard boxes sat on the dining room table with what looked to be their contents, yellowed and dusty, strewn on the chairs and floor. Had he been packing or searching for something? She knew he'd been planning on clearing out the attic once he retired.

There was an open bottle of wine with two of his favorite wine glasses partially full. Did he have company? Were they drinking? Was someone else here when he fell? Why didn't they help him? Were the glasses from earlier in the day, and he was surprised by a thief and attacked? Is that how he became injured? What if that someone was still here?

She stopped her unconscious rocking and looked around the

room to make sure they were alone. Suddenly, the music from the ringtone of her phone broke the silence and made her jump.

She caught her breath when she saw it was Anton and answered. "Hello?"

"CJ, what happened? Are you alright?" His voice was profoundly concerned. They hadn't spoken in hours.

"Oh, Anton, I...I don't know. When I got here everything was dark, but the door was unlocked and cracked open. When I came inside, I found Uncle on the floor!" Candace let out a sob. "He's badly hurt. His head was bleeding, so I placed a cloth against it. He's not moving, but he's breathing. Thank God, he's alive!"

"I will come down." He stated firmly. "I know how you must be feeling, but your uncle is a strong man, CJ."

"No, no! Don't come. I'll be going to the hospital and by the time you get here, it will be nearly morning." Her voice was heavy with stress. "Did you reach Jesse?"

"No, not yet. How long have you been there?"

She hoped she was making sense. "Ummm, it's been about an hour, no, less. When I called 911, they said it would take less than an hour to get here, but they're not here yet. I better call and see if they're lost. I'll call you back. I wish you weren't so far."

"So do I. Call me whatever time. Bye, my кукла." his Russian nickname for her which sounded so playful.

The ambulance arrived moments later, pulling up close enough for their high beams to flood the porch and great room with intense light. Nearly blinded, Candace squinted through the floor-to-ceiling bay window. A couple of police cars pulled in right behind them and uniformed figures immediately swarmed the house. Of course, they would need more time and daylight to scour the entire ranch. EMT's were all over him with needles, wires and machines, accompanied by beeps and buzzes. An endless series of numbers were shouted and relayed over and over into walkie-talkies. Candace was pushed out of the way.

The officer in charge attempted to question Dan but there was no response. He turned to Candace as if on auto pilot. Sheriff Sam Solodad, a native from Gallegos, had played with her when they were kids. They spent time fishing and swimming together in the lake during the summers, and it was widely suspected he had a crush on Candace, but it didn't seem as if he remembered her now.

After telling him how she came to find her uncle and explaining her actions since her call to fire rescue, she excused herself to question the larger, burlier of the three emergency responders about her uncle's condition.

"Well, it's hard to say at this point, ma'am. We're doing everything we can to stabilize him for transport. How old is your Uncle, Ms... uh, is it Kane?" He asked matter-of-factly looking down at the paperwork on his clipboard.

"Fifty-five next month." She could hardly believe it, he was always so young and vital, a fact credited to her.

"Is he allergic to any medicines? Taking any medications?"

"I think he takes something for high blood pressure." Why hadn't she thought to ask this sort of information and keep it written down somewhere? She must seem so poorly informed. "I've been trying to reach his housekeeper."

"Good, good. Can you please accompany one of the deputies to your uncle's bathroom, and check through his medicine cabinet or a drawer in his nightstand? We often find things there that help us," he encouraged her.

She returned with two bottles in hand and gave them to the medic. Not knowing the pharmaceutical purpose of either one frustrated her.

She looked at the name on his ID tag. "Charlie, do you know my uncle?"

"Yes, quite well, ma'am," he answered. "My son has been out to ride the therapy horses a lot in the past few years."

"Oh, I didn't know." She was relieved to have any kind of familiar contact, anybody who could extend some personal consideration and genuinely care about her uncle. Dan had established equine therapy sessions for youngsters with difficulty communicating. They were working with a grant study to report findings as to how the kids interacted with the animals. So far it was a huge success. Her uncle's ranch was a genuine working ranch with cattle and horses, and these days it operated on a skeleton crew, but he was always looking for ways to utilize the resources since he was never one to take his financial blessings lightly. In addition to the treatment program, he was also working with the county utility company testing the value of windmills for many applications.

"Do you think he'll regain consciousness soon? Can I follow you to the hospital?" She felt more comfortable quizzing him now that he actually knew her uncle.

"I wouldn't recommend it. It's against the law to follow an ambulance with sirens, and traveling at our speed isn't safe. You can come to the hospital later or you can ride with us if you'd like," Charlie offered. He looked to the sheriff as though for confirmation.

"No. Ms. Kane needs to be here a little while longer," Sam asserted his authority, although Candace was quite sure she could have demanded otherwise. If she could wrap things up here and get Uncle to safety, she could tell Jesse to meet her at the hospital. Where was she anyways?

A stretcher with belts and blankets appeared. It took three gorilla-sized emergency technicians to hoist him onto the gurney. Moments later her uncle was whisked over the threshold and into the waiting vehicle, which lit up like a Christmas tree against the night. They sped off toward the highway, spewing sand and pebbles everywhere. A cloud of sand particles filled the air, and only silence was left in its wake.

CHAPTER 6

"Uncle, you just have to wake up!" Candace insisted. With the exception of the force of the oxygen pump moving his chest, he was lifeless. The doctors had performed surgery to relieve swelling in his brain and placed him in ICU. Candace was alone with him again. Nurses were scribbling in charts and comparing notes at their station just outside the door to his room.

"I can't lose another person. Not one other single person," she spoke to the room, her words directed more toward the ceiling than to her uncle. Red faced, eyes brimming with tears, she wished her mom was there. "God, what have or haven't I done that makes you want to teach me so many lessons about loss? I've only just begun to live my life and now this. Anton and I are finally getting somewhere with To Dine For Catering. If Uncle doesn't make it, he'll never see us become successful, or see me get married or have children. I need him so much, Lord," she whimpered. She felt her mother's presence, her warm supportive hug and gentle arms. *Is she here with me?*

Candace strolled over to the window. "Mom, you told me a long time ago that God's word says that when His children cry out to Him they will be heard. I am...I am crying out to Him, Mother."

She dropped her head back, her heart-shaped face tilted upward as if an offering to the sky. Her eyes moist, fixed on the heavens, beseeching.

"If I can just have him back, I will never ask for another thing as long as I live, God, I swear." Her voice was almost guttural in nature. She could imagine her mother's answer in her head, "Have faith, sweetheart. God will not take him from you. You must have faith that the doctors are doing everything they can and he will come back to you."

Candace experienced renewed resolve. She breathed in deeply and made a conscious change in course. She began picking up items that were carelessly strewn around, filling her uncle's empty water pitcher, organizing the untouched pudding and juice containers which awaited his recovery and tucked his sheet in around him.

Her uncle's hand, riddled with tape and needle puncture marks rested peacefully by his side. She caressed his pale skin. It felt like him, and aside from the antiseptic, it smelled like him. She kissed the inside of his palm tenderly and collapsed into a chair beside him. She'd stay as long as he needed her.

"Come on, Uncle, you can beat this, I know you can. We can go off somewhere and stay at some wickedly cool resort, dine at some beachside restaurant. You'd love that—we both would."

Before her parents died, Candace and her uncle had limited face time but what they did have was special. They visited each other on birthdays and school holidays or times like when he wrangled Super Bowl box seats or concert tickets for the entire family. They often flew to his hotel destination du jour for Thanksgiving and Christmas. Destination food became a shared interest.

"Remember when we would all go on Thanksgiving weekend jaunts and pig out?" she said, hoping he would respond with a hearty laugh and tease her about it. Uncle Dan often transported the family to locations with five-star menus. True Mayflower descendants, they enjoyed the circumstance of the Thanksgiving holiday wherever they were. They feasted on house specialty items, not simply turkey, but goose and pheasant and endless sides and desserts that Candace, known for dissecting dishes to identify the ingredients before she was even old enough to pronounce them, couldn't wait to make.

In fact, just two months before the awful crash, they had spent Thanksgiving at The Grove Park Inn near the Biltmore estate in North Carolina. Candace was rendered speechless by the opulent quarters in the historic wing of the building with its own private elevator, whose walls and doors were constructed of chain link that exposed the inner workings. She was fascinated by the circa 1900 furnishings, paintings and other décor spread throughout the hallways and guest rooms and the period dining room. Built by Henry Ford and Alexander Graham Bell, it provided Candace with a history lesson books could not begin to tell. This seemed to please Uncle immensely, and to her amazement at the end of that particular trip, most of which were spent in a serotonin and glucose hangover from overeating turkey and sweets, Uncle Dan remembered to mail her the inn's own recipe cookbook.

He might never know that one weekend ignited her desire to become a chef. Candace swept tears away from her eyes pretending to reposition her bangs behind her ears.

Caught up in her thoughts, she failed to acknowledge the whoosh of air from the corridor as the heavy glass door to the room slid open and closed. The blood pressure machine and respirator pump functioned simultaneously in concert with his artificial breaths. A shadow crept over her right shoulder.

"Dawn! You scared the crap out of me. How did you get down here so fast?" Candace was full of questions, but she wasn't very coherent. "I called. Where were you?"

"I just couldn't stand the thought of you being here all alone, especially without Anton coming down. He called me, and we were both worried."

"But I'm not really alone." She nodded toward her uncle, desperate to include him.

"That's true. I was hoping to catch you and find out more about Dan's condition. You were so vague over the phone."

"I didn't mean to be vague. I just didn't know anything...still don't." Candace brushed by her friend and moved toward the other side of the bed. "I'm only alone now because Jesse isn't here yet, but it's good that you came."

"What's the prognosis?" Dawn spoke of Uncle Dan as if he were some sort of object not flesh and blood.

"His prognosis is fair." Candace stiffened. "But I believe he'll be fine. He just has to be, Dawn."

"What do you suppose happened?"

She took Uncle's hand in hers. "I don't know, and I'm too tired to go through it all again. Once Jesse gets here, I'm heading back to the ranch to get some clothes. They tell me the next 48 hours are critical."

"Do you want me to come with?" Dawn offered.

"No, I'll be fine. Besides, I don't think you want to be running around the hospital in day old clothes tomorrow." It wasn't like Dawn to dress so casually for an evening out, almost disheveled. "I thought you and the congressman had a date tonight? You certainly don't look it."

"Oh, it's a long story, but suffice it to say, I got stood up and decided to catch a movie last minute. Are you sure Jesse is coming? Maybe she went to the ranch?"

As if on cue, Candace's cell buzzed. She spoke quickly but affectionately and hung up. "That was Jesse. She's at the ranch waiting for me. You were right."

"You go ahead. I'll sit with him a little while then head out."

Candace started to object but thought better of it. Someone he knew should be there. What if the nurses weren't watching him closely enough? She gave Dawn a hug, kissed her uncle goodbye, and whispered in his ear, "We'll always have Thanksgiving, Uncle."

Checking with the nurse's station on the way out, they assured her he would be constantly monitored in her absence. She left her cell phone number in case they needed to reach her.

CHAPTER 7

It was almost four in the morning, that special time between midnight and the waking when birds, wildlife and most of the world was asleep. Candace loved this time of night. She walked across the parking lot. Her foot falls were silenced by packed gravel. Drawing in a long, deep breath, the first she had taken since her uncle called during the reception, Candace stared at the moon, longing for a star to shoot past so she could make a wish.

"Thank God I didn't wear mascara last night, or I'd look like a raccoon." Candace sighed, catching a glimpse of her reflection in the car window. Still in her chef's coat and work pants with her hair pulled into a dressy up-sweep, she looked dreadful. She hadn't slept in almost twenty-four hours. Pulling the clips and pins from her hair, she sank into the driver's seat and turned the key, which awakened a confetti sprinkling of dashboard lights and chiming signals, assaulting her already overworked senses. She revved the engine. The drive to the ranch would be a long one. It was too late or too early to call anybody, but she really wanted to let Anton know what was going on.

Stopping for a drive-thru meal halfway and getting gas would provide the pit stops necessary to prevent her from falling asleep on the road or becoming dehydrated. Candace smiled. In a recent television episode of NCIS, Mark Harmon's character, Special Agent Gibbs, had told his underling Ziva to keep hydrating (forcing her to drink bottle after bottle of water) so she'd need to go to the restroom later to "dehydrate" and run interference for him. *Boy, could I use an Agent Gibbs and his team right now to help me figure out what happened to Uncle. I'll find out more about what the doctors are saying in the morning. In only a couple hours, I guess.*

The state highway was desolate but oddly familiar, like an old friend. Not thinking twice about the route, the trip seemed like any other except for the feeling of dread which hung over her like a shroud. Almost losing her last surviving blood relative did not sit well with her.

She called Anton.

"Yes?" he answered on the first ring.

"Hi, I found Jesse." Her voice was strained.

"Yeah me too. She's at the ranch. None of your calls reached her because she was at her son's place outside El Paso last night. What's the news?"

"Uncle's out of surgery, and he's stable. They drilled a hole to relieve the pressure in his skull. They're concerned about brain swelling, but he's stabilized now. The next 48 hours are critical."

There was a pause in the conversation.

"Damn it, Anton! Why wasn't someone there with him? If anything happens to him, I'll just..." Her voice broke off in a gulp. She'd been brave until now.

"You had no way of knowing something would happen. No one did. It was an accident." He sighed.

"Well, that's what the police are calling it, but..." Did everyone she loved have to die in an accident?

"I know it's been a long, hard day, but do you think it was not an accident? Did he not fall and hit his head?" he said a bit confused.

She could almost hear Anton wishing she were stabilized too.

"They don't really know. I told you. He was lying on the floor bleeding from his head. The door to the house was wide open." She stopped describing the scene as she could see it too clearly, sending a chill through her body. "Do you realize if I hadn't come down tonight, coyotes might have gotten him?"

Another gap fell in the conversation as they both grasped the possible outcome.

"But you did," he reassured her. "Where were the dogs?"

"The...I don't know. Oh my gosh, I don't remember seeing them. That's really strange."

"Candace, you know I'll come down there if you want. I'm in Denver now." His voice was thick with worry. She knew he would come right down. Hell, he'd scale mountains for her.

"Oh no, you must be exhausted. Did you just finish up?" Her mind snapped back to business for a minute.

"About one thirty. It was a good job. Good tips all around."

The amount of tips collected at the end of a night was a caterer's report card, although not a completely accurate one since it often depended on how much liquor the bridal party consumed. It was still one of the ways she measured success.

"Good. Well, don't come. It's late. Get some sleep, and I'll call you in the morning. I mean, later."

"Okay, if you are really alright, *Спокойной ночи.*"

"That's an expression I don't recognize. What does it mean?"

"Ahem," he cleared his throat. "It means good night. I'm surprised I never told you."

"Oh, I like that. It's pretty. Goodnight."

The car was painfully quiet again. Candace lowered the window and let the cool, dry air work its way through her loosened hair. She was lucky to have met Anton. She wondered if it was sheer luck or divine intervention that their paths had collided. He was born halfway around the world in Russia where his darling *babushka* raised him after his parents divorced and moved to other countries. They lived above her little coffee shop, where he helped her bake and cook and learn an honest trade.

He was packed off to University in Paris where his father insisted he go, but shortly after that he applied to culinary school in the United States with the hope of tracking down his mother and following in his grandmother's footsteps. He hadn't the time or inclination to trust anyone until meeting Candace, and the two had cooked, eaten, and shared nearly every waking moment of the past three years together. Were they attracted to each other? At times, but one or both seemed to hesitate every time a situation arose. She had no clue why Anton held back, but Uncle Dan had cautioned her early on about a division of business and personal relationships, like church and state. However, her own parents had done it successfully. Only time would tell.

When Candace reached the ranch again, it was nearly sunrise. Without the cover of darkness, the iron and wood entrance loomed before her. Veins of lavender and silver streaked the indigo sky that smothered the flat desert, barren with the exception of brush and the occasional Pinon tree or cactus. The lighter shades of sky helped reveal the gates in front of her, currently locked in an open position. The steel windmill and three-story barn with stables stood to the left.

To the right the sprawling log home came into view. It was surrounded by a salmon-pink adobe wall adorned with blue floral ceramic tiles, which created a lovely old-world Spanish courtyard. During mid-day it would be ablaze with brightly colored flowers and towering cactuses encircling an eight-foot-tall triple tier water fountain. It was rare that the fountain was not splashing and bubbling much to the delight of small desert creatures, but right now it was silent like the man who lived there.

A few prairie dogs scampered in front of her headlights. The black, late model Jeep belonging to Jesse was parked alongside the 3-door garage behind a squad car. The front door was sealed with yellow police tape. Candace found a deputy she hadn't met earlier and Jesse talking in the kitchen over coffee.

The officer greeted her. "Good morning, Ms. Kane."

"I guess, if you say so. Personally, I've had better." She smiled wanly and leaned over to brush Jesse's cheek with a kiss. She thought the man looked way too comfortable in one of the high-back, hand-carved chairs. He stood up politely, noticing her hesitation, and shook Candace's hand. She could tell he would have felt more at ease tipping his quasi-western sheriff's hat which lay on the table, rim side up before him. She was familiar with these cowboy types and decided to confront him right away.

"Why is the front door blocked off?" Candace quizzed him. He rose to his feet.

"Well, ma'am the boss wanted to be thorough since you were so insistent someone might have purposefully hurt Mr. Kane. We took some fingerprints, and sent them out but would like to keep people away from the area, just in case," he said nervously, picking up his hat, turning the rim in his hands.

"Thank goodness," she said, letting her breath out and sat down.

Jesse made some of the best espresso in the country, and today she'd need one. The towel used on Uncle Dan's head had been replaced with one with bold stripes, and the sink was as shiny as a new penny. Scrubbed clean with no sign of the blood Candace had washed off her hands. The huge table at the end of the kitchen where they sat was in front of another large bay window, a twin to the one in the living room. An impressive elk horn chandelier hung low over it with tiny light bulbs that could be set to electronically mimic flickering candlelight, as they did now. Guests could look out over the foyer garden through both windows, but from this vantage point, not far from that enormous fountain, stood a cast iron steed reared on his hind legs, mane flying.

"What are the doctors saying?" Jesse spoke, reaching around the deputy to serve him.

Candace briefly explained the ordeal and finished with leaving Dawn in the hospital with her uncle. "He's drugged and sleeping."

"*Dios mio*, that sweet man," Jesse often spoke in what she called Spanglish, a mixture of both English and Spanish. After all these years it was still difficult for Jesse to express great joy or sadness without reverting to Spanish. The house phone rang out. Candace jumped up to answer it so Jesse could finish her conversation with the deputy. Following a brief chat with the head nurse, Candace quietly cradled the phone on its base and turned to look at Jesse. Her face flushed.

"Forgive me, but that was the hospital asking whether we want to place a DNR in Uncle's chart." She took a deep breath. "That's a do not resuscitate order, Jesse. I don't know what to do."

Candace held a hand on her stomach which was suddenly turning somersaults. The chicken sandwich and fries she had eaten weren't faring well. Any decisions her uncle had made about his life and how he would want to be treated were never discussed between them. Uncle was never ill and seemed so energetic and full of life. He exercised regularly and rode his horses all the time. She had no reason to think that an order not to resuscitate him should be in place. Maybe it was naive of her never to have asked, she chastised herself, then said aloud, "Now what?"

Jesse cried out wringing her hands. "Oh, Miss Candace, I know your uncle would no want to live if he could not do it fully."

"I know. But I need to find out what his wishes are. Where would he keep papers like that? In the safe?"

"I think, yes, but I don't know the combination to open it." Jesse broke down unexpectedly. Her head dropped as light sobs escaped. "Oh, what will we do without him?"

Roles played for years were suddenly switched. Candace needed to find a way to comfort the comforter. "Just pray, Jesse.

Don't worry, I'll find the papers." She patted the delicate but strong woman on the shoulder and heaved a sigh.

"Officer, before you leave can you tell me what you know at this point?" Candace turned her attention back to the deputy who peered under the chandelier, squinted against the light and looked anything but comfortable now.

The officer began slowly. "Well, as I said, we've sent finger-prints to the lab and are interviewing anyone who may have seen someone enter the ranch from the highway. We'll be broadcasting some information on the morning news, and we've already got something in the paper."

"Good, did you find any potential weapon except the poker?" Candace wondered if they might have found something she missed.

"Ah, no ma'am. It is possible that your uncle fell and struck his head and someone else opened the door to help him."

"Or he could have opened the door for the dogs, and then...oh my gosh the dogs! That's why it's so quiet around here. Where are they, Jesse?"

"I did not see them when I arrived. I, I thought you had someone take them away for safety," she answered. "¡No! My babies."

The deputy flipped his notebook open to transcribe. "Your uncle's dogs are usually in the house?"

"Yes, yes. They are always with him. They're Great Danes–Merlin and Lancelot. They must have gotten out or chased whoever it was that hurt him." She ran to the patio calling for them and whistling their familiar command. Nothing but silence reverberated back. "Where could they have gone? It's not like them to just take off. They're too well trained."

"I'll call to alert the sheriff," the deputy informed them.

"If you need it, I have a picture of my uncle with them in the den," Candace responded.

"I'll get it for you," Jesse spoke up and gathered herself.

"I can't believe I didn't notice their disappearance. Anton asked me about the dogs a little earlier. I hope they aren't hurt," Candace thought aloud, twisting the ring on her right hand, a habit inherited from her mother. "If you'll excuse me, I need to change into my boots and search the ranch."

Candace ended their discussion and went to the bunkhouse where the ranch hands and stable mates once lived. With staff recently curtailed, she expected it to be empty. The bunkhouse featured clapboard siding fashioned with high windows and makeshift shutters. Although the surroundings were simple, the beds had down comforters and each unit was equipped with a large screen TV. Personal touches were added by the workers, and over the years each dorm room had become homey. Maybe the dogs had spent the night there.

Fragile sunlight streamed over the terrain and between the other buildings. Candace called and whistled repeatedly, disturbing the horses in the stables. She heard them whinny and snort as she passed by. It was dry, and sand flew freely. A couple of the men who still worked the ranch during the day began arriving. One rushed over and grabbed her arms with both hands.

"Miss Candace, I just heard Mr. Dan was rushed to the hospital. What happened?" Riley towered over her as he'd done since she was a girl. He was in his 40's now but looked quite a bit older. His wide brimmed Stetson overshadowed her like an umbrella and covered a full head of chestnut hair that curled out from the inner edge, softening his creased and weathered face. She searched his anxious eyes, trying to find words to tell him the boss he revered had been struck down.

After filling him in on the details and answering his questions, she put him on the hunt for Merlin and Lancelot. "I know we're shorthanded, Riley, but please ask the men to comb over every inch of the place. I haven't slept, and I don't expect I will, but I really need to get back to the house and try to get Jesse to rest."

"Jesse's okay then?"

"She's fine. She was with her son in El Paso. Uncle was here alone."

"Damn it, Candace!" he grabbed his hat off his head and struck his thigh with the rim. Surprise and frustration obviously getting the better of him, he shook his head. "I tried to tell him it wasn't safe to be here without at least one of us."

"I know Riley, I know. Me too. It won't happen again. He'll have someone here from now on after he comes home." She looked down at the toes of Riley's well-worn boots so he couldn't see the pain in her face as she wondered if he would even be able to come home.

"Well, you get yourself some rest, Miss, and tell Jesse not to worry 'bout lunch. We'll be fine with snacks from the fridge. I'll get the guys going," he said.

"Thanks." She walked back toward the house feeling completely spent. A shower would feel great right now.

Candace could hear Jesse in the den exercising her crisis defense mechanism. Jesse dealt with adversity by creating clean and orderly surroundings. Right now, she'd leave her alone as there was no use trying to stop her. Candace made her way down the tiled hallway. Large pictures of Native Americans and buffalo on the plains accented by pinpoint gallery lights hung on each side. The door to the room she'd had as a child stood open. Crisp white curtains blew in the gentle morning breeze. An eyelet comforter covered the bed accented by pillows in rich garden colors. Antique furnishings were sparse: a dresser, blanket, chest, and a single bowl-and-pitcher washstand stood in the corner. Relieved to be surrounded by good memories, she shed her clothes and stepped into a nice hot shower in the adjoining bath.

The unforgettable smell of freshly washed linens and sweet pine filled the room when the steam permeated the logs. The waterfall showerhead spilled a steady sheet of water through her hair. The warmth cradled her shoulders like a grandmother's shawl. She felt a sudden release of emotion and sobbed into her hands and let it all go—the phone call, the seemingly endless drive, the darkness, Uncle's nearly lifeless body, the blood, the sirens, the silence, the hospital, the fear, Lancelot and Merlin.

She had only cried like this one other time.

News of her parent's death had roared through the neighboring towns of North Miami and Little River like the freight trains that rumbled along the southern Florida railway tracks. The loss thread its way through Cynthia and Brad's friends, business associates, and employees as deliberately as the hundreds of sewing machine needles thrashed daily through material at their manufacturing company. All of the equipment was still as it would unfortunately remain. The rumors rustled through Candace's school too, on sheets of lined and folded notebook paper, passed and then discarded. Candace actually saw one of the notes, written by a classmate speculating about how she must feel. Feel? Were they kidding? She felt nothing.

Over the course of the next few days, she'd learn about traditional funeral pomp and ceremony. It was preceded by food deliveries of all kinds and baskets of fruits and flowers. These feeble attempts to convey condolences fell short of their goal. Instead, their home reeked like a combination delicatessen, Italian restaurant, and flower shop.

Uncle Dan had taken care of all the arrangements and whisked her parents from Denver by private jet as soon as the authorities released the bodies. Matching ivory caskets with brass handles were offloaded by a food service lift and spirited away under the cover of darkness. There would be time for goodbyes later in the week she was told, but that night she could only observe at a proper distance; wrapped snugly in her mother's old bathrobe, holding a ratty overstuffed version of Winnie the Pooh, she had let the tears flow.

~

"Candace. Miss Candace. You come right away? The men, they've found the dogs." Jesse was banging on the bathroom door shouting. "Is bad, is bad."

"What? My god, I'll be right there." She twisted the valve, shoved the curtain back and grabbed a towel in one brisk move. It was plush, soft, and welcome, but the feeling was temporary. Wrapping herself in a handy Indian-blanket robe, she ran after Jesse barefoot on the earth like she did as a child.

Merlin and Lancelot were in the arms of Riley and one of the younger, newer hands. They were being carried like one ushers a bride over the threshold, but a bride that had one too many drinks—heads bobbing and legs dangling. The men were hurrying toward one of the pickup trucks.

"Are they dead?" Candace almost screamed the words.

"No Miss, they're unconscious though. We've called the vet but we're meeting him. No telling what's wrong with them. Could be a snake or some kind of poison, maybe. We thought it best not to wait."

"Right, definitely." She reached them just in time to run her hand gently over Lance's large sleek head. Foam was spewing from his mouth. His stiff spindly legs intertwined with Merlin's as they lay in the charcoal-gray vinyl-lined bed.

"You have to be okay, boys. You just have to be." Wiping an escaping tear from her cheek, she backed away and stood with her arms wrapped tightly around her waist.

"Want to come?" Riley looked at her standing barefoot in the robe. She followed his gaze.

"No, you go. I'll be right here, waiting for your call." The truck kicked up a swirl of dirt - as the ambulance had just hours ago.

This was no accident.

CHAPTER 8

L ancelot was returned to the Double K around noon, alone. He was revived and his stomach had been pumped but Merlin, still unconscious, was kept at the animal hospital for more treatment. The initial diagnosis was poisoning.

The vet called Candace as soon as the results of his examination were clear and questioned her as to Dan's possible use of any drugs or the chances of the ranch hands making anything available to the animals either by accident or on purpose. He informed her that he would need to report the evidence of the ingested drugs to animal control for the authorities to further investigate. She told him what had happened the night before and of her suspicions that an intruder meant her uncle harm, it seemed logical to her that someone drugged or sedated his dogs in the process. The vet cautioned her not to jump to conclusions as this could be an unfortunate coincidence.

Lance napped in bed beside Candace, who finally rested. Even Jesse went to sleep after a phone call to the hospital confirmed her boss was stable, resting peacefully with no change in his condition. She and Candace were cleared to visit him that evening. Jesse retreated to her studio apartment off the kitchen, and

Candace sprawled across her bed wondering how everything could feel so normal yet be so distorted. Sleep, although limited, came rather quickly.

The piercing ring of the house phone woke Candace at dusk with the veterinarian telling her Merlin had passed away from cardiac arrest. Was it true or a dream she was having? As he droned on in a subdued tone with details of the pet's demise and arrangements for his return to the ranch, Candace was forced to accept the nightmare was real. She hugged Lancelot tightly by the neck and cried into his short, sleek fur.

The pair had been inseparable, and Uncle Dan spent as much time as possible exercising and training them. How was she going to tell him? Whoever did this was just sick. Candace forced herself to her feet, pulled on a pair of jeans, cowboy boots and a white button-up shirt. Brushing her hair into its simple bob, a touch of foundation and a smudge of peach lipstick was fuss enough for tonight. As she stepped back for a final look, something in her reflection caught her eye. It was her necklace. The single gold-plated aspen leaf, found in her father's coat pocket when his body was recovered, along with a gold pendant of two interlinked initial K's. A gift from Uncle Dan the first Christmas they spent at the ranch without her parents. That was the year they changed the name of the ranch to the Double K.

She liked what she saw and gave herself a quick nod. Life's circumstances may not have been of her choosing but they gave her a reason to adapt and evolve to the point she was as comfortable in these surroundings as she was in Miami Beach or Manhattan, and that's all because of Uncle Dan. No matter what, she would find out what happened, and he would come home! The image she left behind in the mirror tonight was one of a woman who had grown, developed and matured whether she was ready or not. A twinge of doubt tightened her stomach muscles.

She threw a change of clothes and some toiletries into an overnight bag so that she could stay at the hospital. Jesse would be going home after visiting hours, but Candace had been away from him long enough. Maybe her being there will make a difference. The sound of her voice, the touch of her hand might just cause him to wake, she told herself.

Before leaving the ranch that evening, Jesse insisted they both grab a tuna sandwich, which evolved quickly into a tuna melt and fresh fruit salad, since Candace had not eaten. Each taking their turn hugging Lance's neck, they double-checked the windows and doors to be safe, a feeling so foreign in this place of tranquility. Riley had offered to stay in the bunkhouse for a few nights until Dan and some sense of normalcy returned, or they didn't need him anymore. Candace could never imagine not needing Riley around and told him so. They had been family for as long as she could remember.

She couldn't recall ever seeing Jesse cry like she did when they entered the ICU. Jesse stood next to Uncle Dan, his aura devoid of laughter or warmth, and she simply lost it. When she pulled herself together enough to speak, she asked about the tubes and machines and what each of them did.

Candace said softly and steered her from the room, "Oh, Jesse, I never could have seen my parents like this. In a way, I'm glad they died instantly."

Insisting on buying Jesse a cup of coffee before she headed home, they continued to reminisce. It would be over an hour drive to reach the tiny house where she raised her only son as a single mother. Living just a few doors down from her sister all these years made it possible for Jesse to exist in her double role of mother to Pedro, and the Kane family Wonder Woman with an apron instead of a cape.

Jesse's sacrifice, splitting her time and heart between them, started early on. First with impromptu family get togethers in Key West and at the ranch. Uncle Dan and Candace even taught Jesse to ski in Breckenridge. Although her son and husband were invited to join them on numerous occasions, her husband's pride stood in the way of what he called charity. When Candace was vacationing during summers as a young child, Jesse would spend many a rainy afternoon in one of the kitchens, teaching Candace cooking techniques and about the fascinating world of baking. It seemed only fitting that Jesse was the one to accompany Candace back to her empty shell of a house the day of her parent's funeral. The young orphan hadn't been there since the day the limo came to whisk her off to the Keys. The day before the awful truth was revealed. The funeral was held nearby, and she had wanted to take something of her parents with her.

Uncle Dan had met them at the door and said, "CJ, I know this will be hard."

She remembered being grateful that he didn't call her by her given name Candace Jo or worse yet, Candy. She detested that nickname ever since the kids at school grew old enough to taunt, "Candy Kane, Candy Kane, how's Santa?"

She had answered his concern. "I'm okay."

"Well, sure you are. You're from hardy Kane stock," he said biting his lower lip, his eyes glossy. For as long as she knew them, both her father and uncle had been stoic, bordering on distant, something her mother blamed on their Bostonian roots.

Once upstairs, Candace had beelined to her own bedroom. Jesse wasn't far behind. It was different–sparse and empty– though all her belongings and furniture were there. She was told Uncle scheduled movers to pack their personal things and the house would soon be shown by realtors and eventually sold.

"Who will buy it? Where will I go...?" Her words trailed off and with them Candace bolted to her feet. She ran toward the master suite, landing sprawled across her parent's raised four-poster bed which smelled of her mother's *L'air de Temps* perfume. The entire room was layered with peach silk and ivory lace with touches of forest green in the delicately flowered wallpaper and tapestry chair. It was all so much like her mother–absolutely beautiful but solid and strong like the honey pine furniture. Yep, she was both, as people kept telling her.

Jesse had sat down next to Candace on the silk duvet and gently rubbed her forearm. "I wish, oh my Ka-liiinda, I wish to say something, anything that would make you feel good again." Although her English stumbled, Candace could tell she meant every word.

Candace's sobbing ebbed as the words of kindness poured over her. "I have nobody, Jesse." She looked at her with desperation through falling tears. "Do you think he'd let me live with him?"

"I canno' imagine him saying no." She hugged Candace tightly.

But how could Jesse have a clue as to what he thought? Mom and Dad often commented that Uncle was kind of a playboy. He hired Jesse, then ten years and several women, hundreds of dinners and dozens of parties later, he possessed five—no six cars, three houses and a jet. How could she be certain what he would do?

"Let us finish up here and go, yes?" Jesse said reaching for the tissues on the nightstand. "It is in the past, Candacita. You will see that the future will be better, *bueno*."

Candace nodded, blowing her nose, then wriggled free to wander around the room preoccupied and still sniffling. She found a ring from her mother's velvet lined jewelry box—a rather small one, with a single ruby in the center. It had been a gift from Candace for Mother's Day that previous May, bought with babysitting money that took her three months to save.

Before leaving the closet, she stopped at the built-in dresser below the rack of her Dad's neckties. Pulling a drawer open, she chose her favorite pair of his cufflinks. They were gold with a large initial "K" engraved in each. Handed down to him from the grandfather she had never met, they were given to her dad, not Uncle Dan, because her grandmother thought the youngest would be comforted by a tangible, lifelong memento of his father. Candace had realized how her father must have felt. She slid them into her pocket.

"I love you Jesse," Candace whispered as the two embraced, neither one wanting to release the other.

"*Ser fuerte mi amor*, be strong my love," she said. "This too shall pass."

Jesse had promised to always be there for her. Candace's mother had made the same commitment, and even Dawn had solemnly sworn to be by her side on occasions when reassurance was necessary. No one could ever really keep that promise but Jesse had come damn close.

Now, completely alone, sitting on a doctor's adjustable metal stool beside her uncle's hospital bed, Candace was chilled to the bone. This sterile environment wasn't just antiseptic; it was kept at about 68 degrees making a blanket and sweater necessary. The bed was ineffectual at containing his large frame; unable to find enough of an edge to prop herself and be near enough to feel close, she held his hand.

"Uncle, do you remember the months after Mom and Dad died?" Candace spoke with a quiet but hopeful tone, willing Dan to wake up and answer.

"They died in January but by the end of April, you had me seeing a top doc in clinical psychology at the University of Miami. Even though clients hounded you and work piled up, you stayed with me in Florida because the doctor said dealing with delayed grief was serious business." Candace held his hand tightly afraid to let go for a second. "That's what I'm going to do now, Uncle. It's you and me all the way. Do you hear me? You just have to get better. How did you even know back then that I really wasn't okay, that I was reeling from denial and running away from their death?"

The pump of the respirator gasped in an eerie way as if he'd almost said something, causing Candace to jump nervously. She quieted her voice. "I would curl up in bed, not sleep or eat and could barely have a conversation with anyone." Her tear fell on his hand. "Do you remember how tough it was for me to accept help? I wanted no part of it, but you insisted. At one point, I remember you threatened to resort to legal action and confine me in an institution."

There was still no comment from the man who knew everything about her life.

"Remember Uncle? Remember?" She did and always would.

Bringing herself back to the present, she bent over Uncle and whispered in his ear, "But you won, didn't you, dear Uncle?" She kissed him tenderly on his hand; the coldness of his skin repelled her. "It took about six months for me to face my fears. All my pent-up rage and desperate loneliness, but you were there."

Candace felt she needed to keep talking, to warm him to memory and thaw his recollection. She had to bring him back to her somehow. "Remember my counselor, that quirky little man with the shiny bald head and those beady eyes who hid behind the round John Lennon spectacles?" She looked hopefully at his ashen face and closed eyes. Would they open soon?

A nurse came in to check his vitals, "Oh, don't let me interrupt, it's good for patients in a coma to hear the voices of those they love," she said convincingly. "We've seen it do wonders."

Candace blushed, "I was just reminding him about a time when he was waiting for me to recover." She smiled shyly and wiped away a few tears that escaped. The nurse jotted in the chart, moved stealthily about the machines with her sturdy white shoes making little noise. Her existence was nearly undetectable.

Candace continued, "Do you remember Doc Hayward? When he made rounds, he wore those silly loafer slippers, corduroy I think, and that tired cardigan." She smiled and searched for a reaction on Dan's face. "I swore up and down the man had a fixation with that kid's show guy, Mr. Rogers." She grinned sheepishly.

The nurse smiled encouragingly as she left the room but returned quickly, pushing a huge under-stuffed, dark-green vinyl chair, deftly navigating it to the opposite side of the bed. Disappearing again, she returned once more with a piping-hot cup of coffee.

Candace collapsed into the chair, which was superior to the stool. She sipped coffee, and reminisced about the nurses and staff at the rehab center where she spent a good deal of her thirteenth year. It had been a cheerful, peaceful place, established in a refurbished 1920's plantation homestead not far from the ocean. Surrounded by a huge porch, varnished and filled with hardwood rocking chairs, it allowed patients to rock to their heart's content between sessions, accompanied by the whir of hummingbird wings and the harmonious sound of wind chimes in the coastal breeze.

Those mental images made Candace drift into a dreamlike state wondering if it was Doc Hayward's likeness to Mr. Rogers with his soft-spoken demeanor and attentive, inquisitive nature, that gave way to honest and open reflection. Or, was it the odd bird watching, Hitchcockian part of his character that expertly coaxed Candace's thoughts back from the darkened places they dwelled? Regardless, she had successfully climbed from the recesses of despair and gloom, rung by rung, up the rickety ladder of hope. Thanks to him, Candace emerged a young lady who had known fear but fought it. Her wilted spirit blossomed.

Candace fell to sleep stirring only once as that same sweet nurse pushed the chair into a reclining position and covered her with a warm blanket. The caffeinated coffee had little effect on her exhausted and chilly being. It was then she made a promise in the recesses of her mind.

No matter what, she would make herself feel, accept and deal with whatever came to pass and not deny it.

Candace and her Uncle slept to the rhythm of the machines whooshing and clicking.

CHAPTER 9

Anton saw the foyer light on in the To Dine For Catering offices, and Dawn's car parked outside where she usually left it when she and CJ would run off to Lo-Do, a section of lower downtown Denver. As far as he knew, Candace was still in Gallegos so he was suspicious.

He opened CJ's office door and peered into the dimly lit room beyond. "Hello, Candace? Dawn?"

"Yeah, it's me. I'm in the closet," Dawn answered. It seemed strange she was there alone. He thought immediately of the wall safe Candace kept hidden behind her favorite framed poster from the Boston Museum of Art. He didn't trust Dawn as far as he could throw her cat under the rocking chair, or whatever that colloquialism was. Since the day CJ introduced them and Dawn treated him like the hired help, he couldn't shake it.

He flicked on CJ's desk lamp to make sure nothing was disturbed as Dawn emerged.

"I was just getting the dress Candace is letting me borrow for the fundraiser," she said offhandedly.

"How'd you get in here?" Anton responded.

"The light was on, and the front door was unlocked. I knocked, but no one answered. I thought maybe you or CJ were burning the midnight oil, or burning something together," she teased, tilting her head to one side. She threw him a look and winked.

"The door was unlocked?" he asked suspiciously.

"Of course it was. You don't think I'd break in, do you?" She scowled at him and stepped closer. "Now, if I knew you were here alone, maybe I would have given it some thought, Tiger."

Anton was not amused by her flirtatious tone. He had to hand it to her though, Dawn knew her way around a man, any man. She liked switching the topic of conversation, adding innuendo. Was there ever a time when she didn't come on to him, even when Candace was around?

Dawn was dressed to kill, or at the very least, seduce, wearing a tight, off-the-shoulder, red mini dress. It fit her shape so exactly, he was pretty certain there was nothing underneath. The only two things that didn't look painted on her body were the strands of wooden beads dangling from her neck. Her hair was full and windblown. In high heels, Dawn was almost as tall as he was with legs that seemed to travel forever. Tan and doused in perfume, she filled the room with a scent of musk with fruity undertones.

"I stopped because I saw the light and your car but—," he started to explain but she interrupted.

"Oh really? You were hoping to find me here? Now, the truth comes out!" She placed her hand delicately but firmly on his forearm, rubbing it upward to cradle his bicep with her long nails extended. "Don't worry, big boy. I'll never tell. Mmm, I can see why Candace finds you appealing."

Anton didn't say a word. He just stood, tolerating her presence.

"Oooh, the strong silent type. I like that in a man," she said and moved closer to him whispering the last few words in his ear.

"Don't be ridiculous," he said and took hold of both her arms in an attempt to push her away. "Why are you here?"

"I told you, Candace said I could borrow a dress." She used the opening created by his outstretched arms to wriggle free and force her body into him, pressing her hips against his. Before he knew it, both of her hands were on either side of his face, keeping his head locked in place and totally involved while she kissed him on the mouth. Her lips were soft and open, her tongue exploring. He couldn't help but taste her.

His already taught abdomen stiffened, and his hands clenched her arms. He couldn't help but react to her unexpected advance and her insistence. She was smooth and fit and felt hot next to his body—a body, which naturally and inexplicably responded to her presence since he hadn't been with a woman for some time.

As his desire swelled against her pelvic bone, he felt the grip on his head lessen, just as a fisherman might loosen the tension on a line preparing to reel in a big catch. Dawn sucked gently on his tongue, pulling it deeper into her mouth. He wondered if she was aware she was moments away from gaining total control of him. Anton let go of her arms and grabbed her waist. Intending to push her away, he pulled her to his groin instead with both hands. His palms slid easily around to the small of her back. He rubbed himself against her upper thigh. The hem of her tight little skirt slid upward.

Their mouths were open wide, tongues groping for more. He really wanted to stop this, but she was so eager, so damned inviting, and his resolve was slipping. Damn, sometimes a man felt completely out of control! He felt a pulsating urgency to satisfy himself.

She grabbed the back of his neck as he lifted her off the floor and carried her across the room to the desk. Like an acrobat, she flung her head back and arched her body to enjoy the motion of the ride, her bare legs wrapped around his waist. He tightened his hold and pulled her upright as smoothly as an accomplished dancer might embrace his partner's body. The light on the desk revealed the tattoo behind her left ear. So close, he could touch it, a coiled snake in shades of gold and copper with a cobra's head.

57

Anton's eyes flashed fiercely with an intensity that seemed to make Dawn a little uneasy.

She came to rest on the edge of the desk. His hands, no longer needed for support, reached up and slid the neck of the dress off her shoulders revealing her entire upper torso. Braless, as suspected, two perfectly aroused nipples stared back at his glance. He caressed them both like a boy playing with a new toy. Dawn busied herself undoing his belt and breathed in deeply as she slowly unzipped his pants working them and his silky boxer shorts past his hips. They cooperatively fell to the floor, exposing him fully.

Her skin was like satin, smooth and silky. She glistened in the glow of the lamp as he pushed her flat onto the hard, wood surface. He slid her hips toward him preparing to ease himself into her. This American was clean shaven and smooth between her legs. He had to admit, he'd been curious about that. Then, spreading her legs between his strong thighs, he slid his hands around to grasp and control her backside, moving her even closer to him. At last he pushed himself deep inside her with disregard, consumed by the soft, delicate folds of her inner body. Her natural scent enveloped him.

"Oh yes!" she cried out, grabbing his hair in both hands. He groaned and breathed deeply to control his response. She untangled her long legs from around his waist with approval and perched on the edge of the desk.

CJ's desk. Why hadn't he carried her into his own office? He really had to stop this insanity.

As if reading his mind, Dawn slipped her hands between her thighs and caressed him.

Oh hell, he figured she'd wanted to sample what he had for a long time.

With increasing speed and a steady rhythm, he slipped in and slid out. It was all he sensed. He felt her rise and fall with each insertion. Anton was providing her with a wild ride, bareback. She held onto him, digging her nails into his shoulders.

He couldn't help but embrace this feeling of power and command. Damn, it felt great. Young, virile and now bent on self-satisfaction, Anton kept at it. He reached the point of exploding with Dawn begging him to let it go. She had better get her money's worth this time around because it could never—would never—happen again.

Dawn shrieked and shivered with delight. "Oh, you're goooood."

He felt himself writhe and tremble with monumental force. It was over. He stared, first at her, then at himself in the mirror hanging on the wall above the couch. The light from the closet seemed brighter than before. He saw his brow, wet from ringlets of hair dripping onto his nose. His gray-brown, smoky eyes had lost their usual sparkle. Now blank, unfeeling and cold, he withdrew and pushed her away in one motion. All the disdain he felt for himself at this moment filled his expression. Grabbing his clothes from the floor, he stormed out of the room.

"Bastard!" she called after him.

Anton was so pissed at himself; he could barely control his temper. Once in his own office, he picked up a bronze statue of an elk and threw it across the room into the fireplace. He wanted that bitch out of their office, now! Out of his life and out of CJ's for good. What had come over him? Other than the fact that he was just horny, how could he face CJ? How could he tell her? He had to tell her because he was sure that Dawn would—in a hurry and with glee.

Anton could hear Dawn running water into the bathtub in the elaborate en suite five-piece bathroom they had built in Candace's office. Would she really be so bold as to bathe in CJ's tub, he wondered? Knowing that whore, she probably would. What had he done? This one night could end his relationship and partnership with CJ. It wasn't so much that it had happened but with whom. His whole future might really be at risk if Dan were to die and leave her completely alone. Would she give up catering, their partnership, friendship and everything else when they meant so much to each other—over this?

He reached into the mini fridge behind the bar and helped himself to a bottle of his favorite chilled vodka, Russian-made, of course, and decided he would take a drive through the mountains to clear his mind in the fresh air. Taking a couple of quick sips to soothe his anxiety, Anton pulled on his pants and left.

The faster he drove on the nearly empty late-night streets, the more confused he became. Okay, so he screwed Dawn. Why did he feel so guilty? He'd never led Candace to believe that he wouldn't sleep with another woman, but their bond had some unspoken baggage. As close as she and Dan had become to him, he should think of her more as a sister, but he didn't, and he was pretty sure she didn't think of him as a brother. Her face would flush when they teased, and their closeness when tipsy or tired was arousing. *I'm always fighting from kissing her on the lips*, he thought.

Now, would he ever find out what she was truly feeling? Should he take a risk and broach the subject or just find someone to become seriously involved with and forget it? This female interaction stuff was crazy.

CHAPTER 10

Candace stirred with the morning shift change. Once her uncle's vitals were reported and the doctors expressed a conservative confidence, she felt relieved enough to head back to the ranch. The drive was a long one. The third trip alone in as many days. It did give her time to think.

What happened to Uncle at the ranch? Did he have a stroke or a heart attack? If so, why would the poker be in his hands and end up on the floor? Was he going to start a fire? It does get cold enough these late summer nights. But what about the dogs? How could they wind up poisoned and how on earth could they get out of the house? Who opened the door? A friend, a stranger?

Nothing made any sense. She wanted to take pieces of the puzzle—all of the ingredients in the recipe and fit them together. Being a trained chef, she could examine, combine, assemble and create—tools that lent themselves well to getting to the bottom of most problems.

As time passed maybe the doctors would determine if there was a physiological reason for his injuries. Of course having Uncle wake up would help. He'd remember who drank the wine with him. Uncle waking up was paramount. What if he never woke up? She shuddered at the thought. What would become of her life? Would she continue catering? Where would she live? These questions were eerily similar to those from her youth.

Thirty more miles to go.

It was nice that Gallegos and New Mexico as a whole was close to Denver as they were a big part of her childhood, but that wasn't the extent of her travel. Uncle's unfettered access to the company jet afforded them opportunity. Their time spent in Cape Cod was a favorite, and she often thought she would like to settle there. The rocky shores and small seaside towns with wooden wharfs extending into bays and fishing boats bobbing on the tides of the North Sea gave birth to seafood restaurants scattered up and down the coast. Uncle Dan and her dad were born there, and she longed for the belonging she felt when surrounded by the seagulls and salt air.

Her mom and dad were married there, and Uncle had fallen in love for the first time. It was not far from where Dawn's parents, Eric and Marjorie, lived for years. It was also where Eric, and Uncle Dan had begun their first investment firm. They had been so close, in fact Eric was her godfather. Their years of success brought them the money and prestige both families enjoyed. It wasn't until her parents died and their vice president, Pamela Loyd-Everett, manipulated investor's stock portfolios, causing a rift between them. So much had changed. Dawn's mom, Marjorie, and Uncle Dan were the only ones alive now, but Uncle's life was hanging in the balance.

Five more miles.

Exhausted from the drive but resolved to answer some of her questions, Candace was determined to find out what was contained in the boxes and papers strewn about the dining room. She was frustrated with the lack of clues. Candace decided to mentally don a trench coat in lieu of a chef's jacket, and make herself a strong cup of coffee. She hated leaving Uncle alone in that place, but if she could find out what happened and why, at least she could help in some way. Maybe she should buy herself a fedora and a cigar. Uncle would definitely be amused.

~

It was still early in the day with the ranch operating at one quarter its usual commotion. After a few sips of caffeine, she stood firmly near the spot where Uncle had lay bleeding in the wee hours. Conviction tightening her jaw and with her hands on her hips, she surveyed the dining room table. Whoever was here obviously took an interest in the items scattered around. *I'll start there.*

Since no one had yet ruled his injuries a crime, nothing kept her from the area where he had been or the nearby rooms. She walked gingerly so as not to destroy potential evidence and carefully gathered up some file folders from the chair adjacent to the great room. Leaning against the beveled edge of the table, she shuffled through some old receipts, recipes cards and papers that seemed to have been filed away by Jesse at one point.

With the invention of computers and cooking websites, did anyone even use recipe cards anymore? Candace lifted the cover of the first file box and looked inside. It seemed as though someone had beaten her to the contents. Legal pads with engraved stationery and other pieces of paper were askew, file folders pulled out, lying atop the others. Neither Uncle nor Jesse would ever leave things so disorganized.

She spied some newspaper articles about the ranch from back in the day. One had a picture of kids swimming in the pond at the first ever ranch BBQ at the Triple Fork, well before the place was renamed the Double K. The article gave mayoral recognition to Dan Kane and his brother Bradford. Another article included a shot of Dawn's parents, who Candace referred to as Aunt Marj and Uncle Eric with her own mom, Cynthia. Her mother looked gorgeous in a Nehru-collared bright yellow dress and shoes to match. She wore a paisley turban in yellow, orange and lime green tones and big hoop earrings. Candace couldn't help but smile thinking of her mom making a fashion statement in the day and how funny her flower-child look was actually in style again.

More photographs taken of all of them coupled together in group shots, with and without their respective families. There was one of Aunt Marj posed arm-in-arm with Candace's dad, his other arm slung over Candace's sunburned shoulders. Marj was positively fixated on Candace's father, her face flushed and her lips pulled taut. It seemed oddly nervous since it was such a playful and relaxed time. Candace and Dawn were very present in the photos swimming, diving, blowing out birthday candles and enjoying every minute.

Another photo showed both Candace's parents. Brad sat with his broad shoulders, dark wavy hair, and an award-winning smile with Cynthia cuddled close. Uncle Dan and Aunt Marj were caught in the background deep in conversation. The camera had frozen that moment in time. Candace couldn't see Marj's face clearly, but from her posture she seemed awfully sad or tired, and Candace couldn't help but wonder if the two had been fighting.

She put that picture aside and took out several more. Most of the photo subjects were obviously three sheets to the wind and proffered a devil-may-care attitude for posterity. She smiled wanly. So many cherished memories, yet sadly they're all behind them. She tucked the other pictures away and plowed through more papers.

In the bottom of the second box, a stack of letters was wrapped tightly in a thick, red hair ribbon. One a child might have used to tie up a ponytail. She fanned through the letters, holding them by one end, and noticed the return address was the same on every one—Dawn's old house in Connecticut.

Candace jumped as Lancelot knocked against her leg and stretched full length on the wood floor to lie down at her feet. "Lance, you scared me!"

Candace spoke to Lancelot who seemed disinterested. "I wonder why these letters are here, boy? They're from Aunt Marj to Dawn the summer before Uncle Eric died. I didn't even know she wrote to Dawn. She called her often enough."

Candace pulled a letter from the pile and opened it.

My darling Dawn,

I know this is not the way you should find out what has been going on, but I can't face having you come home without me here and not know why. Dad and I have separated. Please understand this has nothing to do with you. It has been a long time coming. I wanted you to know before I came to see you next weekend and not just spring it on you then. Please make sure we can spend time together just the two of us. I don't want to discuss this in front of Candace, her Uncle or other guests. Okay, baby? I'll explain everything then.

Love, Mom

What the heck? Separated? That's impossible? Dawn's parents were never divorced, Candace was certain of that.

She extracted another letter which began:

Dawn,

I do wish you would not blame your father for our troubles. It's not your dad's fault. We have drifted apart, and I am sure you now realize, since you're such a mature and grown up young lady, it's very hard to pretend to love someone when you don't. Daddy and I love you dearly, but we are not making each other happy anymore. We're going to get a divorce. Please Dawn, come home before going back to school and we'll talk more about it. I don't want to discuss this on our party weekend.

Kisses, Mom

How heartbreaking for Dawn to get these letters while away from home and not know what to do. Why didn't she ever tell her?

Candace poured herself another cup of coffee, plopped down in the big end chair and opened several more letters. All of them pleaded for Dawn to understand. Her mother's desperate attempts to talk through written words, not on the phone, and certainly not around their families were clear.

She looked down at Lance. "Here I thought we were all so close, buddy. I guess our parents had secrets from us."

His big black nose ventured upward, sniffing the papers in her lap, and then he dropped back into position. "Thank God emails are computer generated, read and deleted today, boy."

One envelope's corner was bent with a letter half out of its sleeve. Candace pulled it out and opened it.

Dear Dan,

As we discussed, I'm leaving Eric before the summer is over. I can no longer bear to live a lie and I want a clear conscience. I have a chance to finally follow my heart. You know it's been over for Eric and me since before Dawn was born, so you shouldn't be shocked. I just can't turn my back on the Kane magic anymore!

What the...? What was she telling Uncle Dan, and how on earth did it get in here with Dawn's personal letters? She flipped the envelope over and rifled through the others to see if there was another letter, or even better, a date stamp. The envelopes were pretty faded.

Aunt Marjorie was leaving Uncle Eric? What was this crap? Over since before Dawn was born? And the most shocking statement of all– "I can't turn my back on the Kane magic?" Was she kidding? Dawn's mother and Candace's Uncle Dan? What on earth was going on?

Candace stopped. It was time to change beverages. She poured herself a glass of wine from the bar, took a sip and then one more for good measure and continued to read, her eyes misting over.

Please make my excuses to everyone this weekend. You always have everything under control. Please don't worry. My secret is safe. But one favor please, if you honestly don't think there is a future for us, please be straight with me, I need to know for my own sake and Dawn's.

You're my rock, M

"Uncle Dan was Aunt Marjorie's *rock?*" Candace burst out. The sharpness in her tone brought Lance to his feet.

Candace sat stunned, her hands clutching the letter. The envelope dropped into her lap. Okay, so Aunt Marjorie told Uncle Dan that she was leaving her husband for him? Did he love her too? Did her dad know? Did Mom? She guessed Dawn knew since these letters were in with hers. This was all too bizarre.

Candace blinked to clear her vision and lay the letter on the table like a specimen as if to examine it for fingerprints. She raised the envelope up. The light of the chandelier illuminated a blue circle impression next to the stamp.

Oh my god! The letter was written the summer before Mom and Dad's accident. That next winter they died in that dreadful car wreck, and the following October, Uncle Eric killed himself. She looked at Lancelot who peered back with questioning eyes.

"That was an awful year, Lance." She guessed Uncle Eric didn't divorce Aunt Marjorie, but ended up killing himself instead. Was it because of Uncle Dan? She had a sudden urge to pick up the phone and call her uncle. She mentally checked herself. Her uncle —as the tabloids were known to say—was "unavailable for comment."

Wow. Dawn and Candace were both in school back then. Later she'd thought they were finding it impossible to concentrate because of the accident. No wonder Dawn was so into drugs, partying and sex with guys!

Candace stared into Lance's eyes as one would a crystal ball. It was late afternoon and the wine had gone to her head. She hadn't eaten since breakfast, and she started to fold like a house of cards. She put the letter back in its sleeve and noticed something faintly written on a smudge of lipstick on the back. The name Dan in bubble letters written by Dawn in that poofy style she always liked, but with a magic marker X drawn through the middle of them. Had Dawn read this letter when she was fourteen and reacted to it in this fashion?

Candace had a million questions. The room began to swim. She folded the letter into quarters and fit it into her shirt breast pocket along with the photograph she had set apart.

With numb fingertips and a chill through her body, Candace shuffled into the kitchen and opened a can of tomato soup. Jesse would cringe, but she was in need of something quick, warm and comforting. She poured it into a coffee mug from the nearby tree stand and nuked it in the microwave. Jesse had been against owning one of them for the longest time. It contradicted her formal chef's training, but she finally caved at Uncle's insistence.

Grabbing a package of saltines from the pantry, she perched on a stool and stared into the cup. She felt thirteen all over again, feet dangling towards the floor, emotions raging, yearning for answers, and wishing her mom was there. The kitchen fell dark with the setting sun.

~

C andace crawled into Uncle Dan's king-size bed, taking more reading material and Lance with her. She knew they both could smell him. She climbed under the masculine honey and chocolate-colored patchwork comforter. Each quilted block of crushed velvet and suede fabric was trimmed in skinny strips of brown leather, the longest of which hung free at the ends of each row creating fringe. Candace dozed off rereading the letter from her pocket.

Her eyes opened to frail veins of sunlight revealing more letters and pictures spread around the room. It was clear Uncle Dan had been rummaging through the contents of the attic. Had he found what he was looking for? And if he did, what was it?

Candace stretched under the sheets, stiff, tired, and confused. Could Dawn's mother have been in love with Uncle Dan and kept it a secret all these years? Even after Dawn and Candace had both grown, living lives of their own? Was this secret accompanied by perpetual lies held only from her? Why on earth? She wondered what Aunt Marj would have to say.

The sun rose enough to shine between the wooden shutter slats. An hour more and the room would be brightly lit. The earth tones and dream catchers hanging in Uncle's room screamed Navajo. Wind chimes just outside his window made from turquoise, lifted one's mood and spirit with a tinkle from the stones. His view of the rock garden beyond was filled with flowering cactus. Several offshoots planted in clay pots, dotted around the interior of his room. Cinnamon-colored tiles covered the floor. Candace needed slippers to protect her feet from the rough edges of the grout and the chill, even in summer.

The house phone rang out, startling her. She was afraid to answer it. "Hello. Kane residence."

"Candace, is that you? It's Tripp."

"Oh." This was a blast from the past. She hadn't expected to hear from her college flame. "Yes, it's me."

"I just heard from my dad about the accident. If you need anything, anything at all, I can come out. I'm living in Colorado Springs, and I've been working with my dad in his law office. Anyway, this is such a shock. I know you must be devastated. Dad asked me to take a look at Dan's will along with any other paperwork you might need. I called the hospital and gave them your uncle's DNR, and I also contacted a couple of specialists back east. I can't imagine the doctor's there in Gallegos are anywhere near the cream of the crop, and I can get someone flown out." He finally took a breath.

Whoa, boy! You've obviously been awake for a while or had a hefty shot of espresso —too chipper for this hour in the morning, she thought but said, "Tripp, how are you?"

"I'm good. It's been a long time," he answered.

"Yes, it has. I didn't even know that you were living here in Colorado. Listen, I really appreciate your offer of help, but I'm leaving today to go back to Denver. I have some business to handle. I can come by your Dad's office another day this week. Will that work?

"I guess so, but be sure to drop by my office when you come in," he said.

"Umm, okay. I'll see you then."

That was Tripp. After all this time.

She had met Tripp the year before he started law school when she was only beginning to ponder the possibility of a career wearing an apron and billowy white hat. Both attended the University of Colorado in Boulder. The city located at the base of the foothills of the Rocky Mountains was home to the oldest and first university in the state.

Drawn by Candace's culinary prowess, he and half the Kappa Sigma fraternity welcomed her late-night study snacks. Nothing spelled comfort food better than bites of Welsh rarebit on toast points or Reuben pretzel nuggets or generous helpings of cheesy grits topped with over-easy eggs and buttered toast the morning of an exam.

As a little sister of the "house," Candace had a knack for sensing a brothers' empty stomach, and it wasn't long before she regularly satisfied Tripp's gnawing study hunger in exchange for time spent entertained by his way with words and soothing logic.

"You see everything so simply and succinctly," she had praised him one evening, sitting on the couch in the Kappa Sigma parlor. Listening to him talk about the state of the country and the world at large, she felt calm and safe. The room was literally old-school with historically important oil paintings and built-in bookshelves enclosing the period furniture. A huge fireplace warmed the room when necessary and telescoping reading lamps were scattered freely to create cozy study corners within the main portion of the area.

"Well, life can be pretty simple and succinct if you choose to live it that way," he'd boasted.

"Not in my experience. Life comes full steam ahead, and if

you're sharp enough, you might just steer out of the way!" she said emphatically. From what she knew of him, both of his parents and his three sets of grandparents were still alive. What would *he* know about loss or loneliness?

"Stick with me, honey, and I'll steer you through the shark infested waters." His tone deepened, creating a dramatic response.

"Thanks, but it's not the sharks I'm worried about. I'd just turn 'em into sushi." She smiled, waving an imaginary knife in the air. Suddenly changing her choreography to a mid-air Hitchcock *Psycho*-stabbing gesture, she added, "It's the unexpected curves and dips in life that'll get ya."

"What's got you so jaded?" He looked over the top edge of his tortoise-shell framed glasses. He obviously only needed them for reading, but they made him look pretty distinguished. He had a copper glow to his hair that matched the richly colored draperies in the room. With golden skin and soft brown eyes, he reminded her of an Irish setter, cuddly and content. She took pride in just knowing this handsome young man, who only broke from relentless studying when she brought her food offerings.

"I just know what it's like to have the proverbial rug pulled out from underneath you, that's all," she stated.

"What rug knocked you on your ass?" He seemed genuinely interested but a little callous.

"My parents died when I was young," she said tentatively. He was surprisingly easy to talk to, but she didn't like sharing the details of her past with anyone.

Pulling his glasses off, letting his book fold into his lap and resting his elbows on his knees, he sat forward and touched her thigh. "I'm so sorry. What happened if you don't mind my asking?"

"They were killed in a car accident when I was thirteen." She hesitated and then went on. "They'd been on a skiing trip. Their car ran off a mountain road in the winter of '88."

"That's awful. You were so young."

"It's not something I dwell on, but when I meet someone who looks at the world the way you do, so comfortably and securely, I can't help but wonder how. I'm always waiting for the other shoe to drop."

"Well, I guess you were adopted by a nice family. I mean, you don't look like you live the life of an orphan," he said, giving a nod to their surroundings.

Could it have been the ladies gold Rolex watch on her wrist or the Burberry scarf around her neck that gave her away?

"No, I didn't. My uncle raised me, my dad's brother. He was there to pick up the pieces when my parents died. He really didn't have much choice since it was written in their will, giving him legal guardianship." She hugged her knees against her chest. "He was a confirmed bachelor, an investment banker from Denver, and like a duck out of water when it came to kids, but we managed. You might know of him—Daniel Kane."

"Dan Kane? Whoa, little lady, your uncle travels in lofty circles. My father's law firm deals with his brokerage house. Dan Kane's little girl...well, what do ya know about that?"

She could see his interest pique. Like many of the other college guys he probably thought she was pretty in a preppy sort of way, smart, *and* wealthy. She knew what came next...the big pick up line.

"So, tell me about you," she countered. Uncle Dan told her that men have two favorite subjects...sports and themselves.

He straightened his back and sat taller. "I'm an Air Force brat. My father and mother traveled all over Europe and Asia when I was young. We ended up in Colorado Springs in base housing for high school. Everything about my life was pretty regimented and planned out for me." He clasped his hands behind his head and rested his back against the sofa arm. "My grandfather served in World Warr II and went to law school on the GI Bill. He founded our family's practice. My dad was expected to serve our country and follow suit, which he did. Now, it's my turn."

"You've been in the service?"

"No, not yet, but I plan to enlist after law school. My dad's a bit of a throwback. He thinks I should get my degree through the Air Force but I really want to go to Harvard."

"Ivy league boy, huh?"

"Hardly, but it's been a dream of mine since I was a kid." He showed a perfect gleaming white smile which almost made her reconsider her decision not to get braces. That tiny space between her two front teeth, though barely noticeable, made her smile less than perfect, but she loved keeping that little part of her dad alive by refusing to adjust hers. She ran her tongue over the gap.

"How about you, what are you in for?" His eyes searched her face.

"Liberal Arts." She shrugged. "Certainly not my dream, but it was something to study. My parents wanted me to go to college. Something about my dad being a self-made man, never having the chance, and my mom was headed for a career in clothing design until she met my dad. The two started a manufacturing business in Florida instead. I was born shortly after, and I'm told they wanted me to have broader horizons." She made finger quotes in the air to punctuate the last two words.

"So, are you into design like your parents or planning to work with your uncle?"

"Actually, I'm starting culinary school next semester. I've always wanted to be a chef." She grinned, tilting her head toward the large empty platter on the coffee table.

"I should have known. You already do pretty well in that department. You can cook for me anytime." He paused to clear his throat and fiddle with his glasses. "Where will you study?"

"I was thinking Le Cordon Bleu in Paris but my uncle twisted my arm so I'm going to Johnson and Wales University in Miami, right near where I grew up, and not far from our place in the Key's."

"Pretty far from Colorado," he commented.

I'm fine with that. I think it's pretty cool that Johnson and Wales were women who founded the school in the early 1900's. How forward thinking was that? Anyway, I think he'd rather I stay close and take short trips abroad to study my craft every summer. When I'm trained, he's promised to help me open a restaurant or something, If I didn't know better, he's afraid he'll miss me." She snickered.

"I can see why," he said agreeably.

Her heart skipped a beat.

"I'd miss your cooking if I were him," he winked quickly and easily as if it came automatically.

She blushed and bent over to gather the platter and napkins to hide her embarrassment. Tripp got up to help. "May I walk you back to, uh, wherever?"

"You may." She curtsied ever so slightly, making fun of his formality. Her family had always been jokesters, not nearly so stiff.

"Harrelson James Long, *the third*, at your service, ma'am." He clicked his heels lightly. "But everyone calls me Tripp."

"The third? Wow, how nice for you. Tripp, hmmm. That's cool. I'm Candace. Candace Kane."

"Candace Kane. Wait a minute...Candy Kane?"

"Not if you want me to answer you. My friends call me CJ. My full name is Candace Jo."

"Well nice to meet you, CJ."

Dropping off the tray and emptying the trash was a prelude to taking a walk on the lush commons lawn that pre-fall evening. Removing his jacket, Tripp made a place for them to sit in front of the college's gothic Old Main building. Under the moon and stars, they peeked through the poplar, maple and willow trees that blanketed the campus. The night sky was clear for miles and rivaled any planetarium. Like wisps of fireplace smoke on the wind, their thoughts about life were propelled to the stars. They discussed dreams that had materialized, remunerated those gone unfulfilled, and contemplated those yet to come to fruition.

When it seemed as if they could no longer communicate with words, they sat holding hands, fingers intertwined like shoelaces snuggly crisscrossed together. Candace gazed at the stars, her back against his chest.

That night, in the beauty of that moon, he told her things she had never heard before. He complimented her beautiful eyes, her high cheekbones and delicate nose as he let his finger follow the pattern of freckles that danced across it. He told her she had luscious lips then kissed her. Their playful banter extended beyond conversation. She welcomed his tongue.

Time escaped them both until he was forced to rush back to the frat house to collect his books as the grandfather clock in the foyer struck two.

The following night, they snuggled by the fire while he studied. The late September coolness and the age of the building gave a chill to the air. Candace had produced a meal of chicken Marsala, angel hair pasta and sautéed asparagus from a single burner hot plate and microwave.

"What are you studying?" she asked.

"Something not in my engineering curriculum, but I'm getting a head start on my law degree."

"What is it?"

"Torts." He chewed on the end of his glasses.

She let loose a teasing laugh. "No silly, it's me who studies torts."

"No, really. Torts are what they call broken laws, crimes—what people go to jail for."

"Oh. Well, the only ones I know about are pastry shells filled with fruit or meat."

Tripp hugged her closely. "That's what I love about you...you are so innocent and untarnished by life. It scares me how perfect you are," he said.

She just smiled. She felt the same way.

It had only been two weeks, but Candace felt comfortable and secure in his arms. It was as perfect as a well-made béchamel sauce. His touch was gentle. She wondered if this could be the way her mom had felt about her dad. As he talked, she absorbed every word. For the first time since her father died, she felt completely safe. His breath drifted against her cheek. She caught his gaze, his eyes devouring her features. His kiss was slow and purposeful, steadily and rhythmically lulling her into another dimension.

An unfamiliar tingling, a longing, crept through her body and made her heart beat rapidly. She wrapped her arms around his neck and brought him closer while feeling her independent nature peel away like layers of skin off an onion. She could love this man more than anything or anyone. She was surprised.

The next day, Tripp buried himself in his books. Law was a jealous mistress, he told her fleetingly when they crossed paths on the same campus green where their lips first touched. He seemed cold and distant. She felt the rug fly out from under her, and felt that other shoe drop. Tripp's classes usurped him. Out of the blue, he pulled away, and she wondered if he too could see his well-organized future disappear into obscurity like one of the dried and tattered leaves upon the wind.

Without another word between them, Candace began her formal transfer early to Johnson and Wales. Instead of starting the next year, she arranged to transfer late into their fall term. Better late than never she told herself.

CHAPTER 11

J uggling hospital visits, the running of two businesses, both hers and the day-to-day responsibilities of the ranch was taking its toll and trying to piece together facts vs. theory about what happened to Uncle Dan was difficult. Candace screened what felt like a hundred calls this morning from his associates, clients, other brokers, even newspaper and tabloid reporters who jumped into the fray. Although semi-retired, Uncle sat on the board of several companies, and they wondered when he could return to the boardroom. The hardest queries to answer were from concerned former employees and his close friends. When would he be well? Next week...next month...ever?

Her own concerns, the typical inquiries about events, operational issues within the world of catering, and her problem-solving talents were put on the back burner. Thank God for Anton. He was ready and willing to handle brides, event planners and even the vendors while Candace read emails and accepted condolences from friends frantic with worry. They questioned her relentlessly but she had no answers. "No change," was all she could say.

This, the third morning of the ordeal, was no different except for the fact the 48-hour critical window had come to a close, and there were no signs of increased danger. She drove the distance into town, coordinating a mind full of details as the miles clicked away on the odometer. If people only knew what it was like to be a caterer, they might come to realize their cost could never really begin to compensate for the hours invested, not just the physically demanding on-the-job hours, but the mental jumping jacks necessary in preparation as well. She really needed to be home and on top of things but with Uncle still unconscious, she didn't see how.

Today would be the culmination of specifics painstakingly noted to files or stored on her computer like dates, times, tastings, site visits, information on the bride, groom, attendants, contact phone numbers, seating charts, table placement and vendors galore. Rentals, cake, flowers, photographer, and music all need to be confirmed. Checklists were made, staffing scheduled, and inventory all ordered days, even months ago.

This was the magical timeframe before an event when everything started to pop. Anton said he found it exhilarating and compared it to a space launch with all systems "go." The menu took on a life of its own, causing them both to shift into high gear and her performance anxiety to peak.

Today a new bride and her mother were expected to go over linen and dish ordering, a fundraiser was scheduled for Friday night, and a brunch wedding reception on Sunday rounded out the week. All of the preliminary work done months before could be for naught if she was kept from holding the reigns. However, that had never happened before. She performed through weather, fever, hangover, broken bones, even surgery, once in a wheelchair, another time hopped up on pain killers, but she always attended her events.

Hands-on involvement was critical, especially when food stuffs were delivered. The storage of groceries and perishables, refrigerated and frozen items, dairy products and fresh herbs, left little if any margin for error in the handling process. Proper temperatures both in cooking and preserving food were an absolute must. Fresh fruits, vegetables and dry goods, each with a different shelf life had to be protected or the company's bottom line would suffer. Throwing away spoiled or questionable items made it impossible to control the ever-elusive culprit–food cost percentages. Tomorrow prepping would be set into motion without her. Food would be chopped, diced, mixed, seasoned, beaten, blended and tucked away safely, she hoped, until the big day.

Candace pulled her car into the hospital's now familiar parking lot, turned the steering wheel with one hand, held her cell in the other, and squinted against the sun. Today, she needed to get in and out in a hurry. She was no less worried about Uncle but felt compelled to return to Denver.

Thankfully, Anton had answered her call on the first ring last night and did his best to convince her to stay where she was.

"I can handle this, CJ. You don't need to worry. I've got this, as you Americans say." He was teasing her but she could hear the concern in his voice.

"I know you can, Anton, but I have some appointments I hate to cancel, and I can't do anything here with Uncle, except watch him breathe." Her voice caught on the last words. "Besides, you can always use another pair of hands."

"Well, take your time. We finished prep on the lamb last night and made all the sauces and dressings ahead. So, we are good to go," he said confidently.

"Oh, how did the recipe for the new rub come out? I was afraid that not using mint would make it flat." She easily switched gears reversing into her comfort zone. Work had always been a haven.

"The rub turned out great. I seared off a piece for dinner last night with the shallot and mushroom sauce. It was perfection. You've trained me well, master Yoda." She could hear him grin. He loved Star Wars, sometimes calling her Princess Leah, and she would refer to him fondly as her Darth Vader.

She was comforted by the satisfaction in his voice. "Good, that's good."

"I will see you tomorrow then?" Anton asked.

"Yes, yes around three. Bye, Vader!" She hung up before he could even ask how Dan was.

Sheriff Solodad's squad car was parked at the emergency entrance again. He was certainly making a habit of appearing at the hospital like clockwork. Freshly shaven, his skin smelling of the sea breeze and glowing from a recent shave, the sheriff would either be in the parking lot or ICU corridor dressed in his standard issue tan uniform, pressed, creased, and crisp against his toasted-coconut tan body. Today he met her at the elevator.

Two insulated cups of strong-smelling espressos in a take-out holder were balanced in his hands along with one pineapple and one guava pastry. She wasn't sure which one was his favorite, but he brought both, so she took the Guava. "How are you feeling this morning Ms. Kane?" he asked with proper formality when she joined him in the elevator. The sliding doors shut out the hospital lobby. "I hope you were able to get some rest."

"I did, but I still had trouble staying asleep. And please don't call me Ms. Kane, Sam."

With the Sheriff in tow, her high heels clacked on the linoleum floor as she made her way to ICU purposefully looking at her reflection instead of peering in at the patients. Her freshly washed hair was clasped back, but without makeup she looked a bit drawn. Sheriff Sam pulled open the door to Dan's room with two fingers, and Candace dropped her briefcase, newspapers, magazines and date book on the only chair in the room before approaching Uncle Dan's bedside.

She reached out tentatively, touching Dan's forehead, gently brushing back a few pieces of soft gray hair. She surveyed his face for any sign of life. His eyelids were still. The only movement in the room for the past two days was that of his breathing, forced by the respirator. He was pale, almost ashen. She held his hand and dropped her chin against her chest.

"Who could have done this to him?" she mumbled softly in despair. Collecting herself, she asked, "What have you found out, Sheriff?"

"That's one of the reasons I'm here. I came to tell you the fingerprints lifted from the door and the house all belonged to your Uncle, the maid, the ranch foreman, you and some friends of your family, no one else."

"Sheriff, Jesse is not a maid. What's the other reason?" She turned off the continuously vibrating phone on her hip.

"Excuse me?" His brow furrowed.

"You said, one of the reasons you're here. What are the others?" she asked quietly, taking a small bite of her pastry. She loved guava. She had eaten it many times before after being introduced to it in the Caribbean as a child.

"Uh, well, before you left for Denver, I wanted to make sure you heard it from me personally, and I wanted to check in on him," he said, nodding toward the bed respectfully then lowering his eyes.

She felt small. "I see."

So, his visit was two-fold—an update on developments in the case, making sure she understood there was little evidence of wrongdoing and to find out about Uncle Dan's condition. She didn't care whether he believed her or not, she knew the injury wasn't an accident.

"Did you find any other weapons? Could he have been hit with that poker?" She blinked away tears to focus her eyes. The entire room was bleak and chilly.

"No, no ma'am, we didn't. He could have been picking up the poker off the floor and hit his head on the stone mantle as he stood, knocking himself out. We are still waiting to hear from the doctors to see what seems most likely. Since they had to perform surgery at the site of impact, we may not be able to prove he was hit with the poker or not."

"Oh Sam, don't ma'am me," she snapped. "I'm sure someone hit him with the poker!"

"I'm beginning to agree with you, but I wish I had something more to go on...anything. We did get some impressions of fresh tire tracks coming up to the house, but they were run over by your car and then the ambulance." He grabbed the Danish and took a big bite.

"So, someone else was there. Could I have disturbed the only clue we had?" She turned to look at Uncle, a man she would protect with her own life. Now she could barely help him.

Sam shrugged. "I suppose so, but they could belong to anyone."

"I'm sure someone was with him, and they just left the door open after he was—" She choked. "—after they hit him."

"We didn't find anything missing and his money and credit cards were still in his wallet, so we're not thinking robbery, but—"

She interrupted him. "Maybe he scared them, tried to fight them off. After all, he can be quite imposing you know."

"He sure can be." He took another hefty bite of his pastry, chewed, swallowed, and then continued, "We're not done, CJ. I'm still looking into what happened to the dogs. So far we have no leads but I'm sure we'll get to the bottom of this."

"I hope so, Sam. I just want him to wake up and talk to me, to tell me that I'm sweating the small stuff." Candace looked at Sam with pleading eyes. "I can't lose him, too."

Sam's face showed genuine concern. He'd known Dan and Candace for a long time and it was no secret how much he admired her uncle. It must have pained him to see Dan's large frame diminished by the mechanized hospital bed covered in bleached white sheeting and his form draped in a pastel green gown. The tubes running out of his body were nothing compared to the wires that hooked him up to various machines.

Sam shifted his weight and placed the pastry and coffee on an empty rolling cart to his side. He took off his hat and tucked it under his arm, revealing his short-cropped jet-black hair. He stood erect, almost at attention, his stance reminiscent of a matador at the ready should a bull try to run him through.

"I hate to be the one to ask this, CJ, but did you and your uncle have any problems, any disagreements?"

"What?" she turned to face him.

"Look, it's standard in this type of situation to question the person or persons who made the initial discovery. It's nothing personal, it's my job, Candace. My understanding is that your uncle let you borrow quite a large sum of money for your catering business. Did you ever argue over that?" He looked at her evenly and waited for a response.

"I really can't believe you're asking me this," she said. "Uncle and I have never had any problems, and he didn't loan me the money. I had to arrange to pull some money from the trust fund my parents set up for me before they died. I'm not entitled to withdraw funds until I'm thirty, and my uncle is the executor of the estate."

"Oookaaay." He drew the word out as he thought on his feet. "Is there anyone that you can think of that would want to harm him?"

"Everyone loves him. You know that," she said, shaking her head.

"Well, let me know if anything or anyone comes to mind," he said officially.

"So, you don't think this was an accident either? It's about time. Maybe we can finally get something done around here."

Sam was noticeably uncomfortable with her present demeanor and took a longer than normal pause.

"What Sam? What's going on?"

"Nothing really," he said, scratching the back of his neck. "I was just thinking about how generous and kind your uncle is–all the BBQ's he would host on the Fourth of July. I was remembering how he always called you 'one of the brightest stars in the sky.' He really loves you, Candace, and I don't want you to be offended. I'm just doing my humble sheriff's job."

Candace sighed. She didn't mean to be short with him. She wasn't the vibrant and happy young girl who led her friends on shopping expeditions around town. She wasn't the Candace he remembered who brought decorated holiday cookies and chafing dishes full of food to the senior center. Life had a way of changing all that, and what mattered now was to get to the bottom of the situation.

At one time she and her Uncle Dan were pillars in their community, positive, supportive and generous, but now with Dan hanging on to life, it seemed the whole town was distraught.

"I guess I'll be going now," Sam said softly.

Candace responded, "I just can't imagine life without him."

"I know how you feel. I can barely let myself think of that either." Sam donned his hat, grabbed his cup, and walked out the door.

"Thanks for breakfast," she called after him.

CHAPTER 12

I *could lose him*, Candace told herself as she drove across the
New Mexico countryside toward Colorado. She had left strict
instructions at the hospital to be called if there was any change.

It was midday. As far as the eye could see, the desert was
bathed in sunlight, a warm, pale-yellow glow which emphasized
the cream-colored sands. It reminded her of a butterscotch
pudding parfait with whipped cream clouds floating atop the
layers. The occasional sage brush rolled across the road, and there
was nothing else for miles to distract her thoughts. Normally this
would be a welcome scene, but it was certainly driving her insane
today.

Speaking with Anton twice, and touching base with several
clients helped pass the time before she arrived in Denver. A brief
detour to the nail salon for fills became a pedicure as well. As was
her practice, Candace arrived at the venue of her next event early.
She couldn't remember driving there, but she had the good
fortune of knowing the city streets and shortcuts like the back of
her hand. Who needed GPS when you worked a venue so
frequently?

Grant-Humphrey's Mansion was built in 1902, on a parcel

of land smack dab in the middle of what would become down-town Denver, tucked among yards of lush trees, plants and flowers. The entire estate was fit for the likes of its former occupants; Colorado's third governor James Benson Grant, and a wildcat oilman and philanthropist, A.E. Humphreys. Since 1976, it had been rented out to everyone from brides to busi-nessmen for special events. A magnificent building, it featured a crescent shaped marble staircase flanked at the front entrance by an elegantly curved veranda of carved stone surrounding the entire first floor. It was a neoclassical wonder surpassed only by the golden domed capitol building just blocks away.

From her perch on the wrought-iron settee, Candace had a birds-eye view as Dawn skidded, brakes squealing to a stop, in her lipstick red, late model corvette. She slipped out of the low-slung cocoon, her long legs announcing themselves first, since her slender black pencil skirt had slid high on her thighs, and her snug scoop neck cable-knit sweater showed off her proudest assets to a tee. Dawn somehow had managed to attain something memorable from every relationship, but the augmentation of her breasts was by far her *coup de grâce*. Candace laughed at the silli-ness of it.

Dawn navigated her way up the stairs and under the great portico, which had been designed to give the front of the three-story house a regal appearance. Dawn's salon-finished long black hair and dark brown eyes gave her an air of Cleopatra. Candace had to hand it to her, wherever Dawn went, she turned heads. The gardeners and painters were her audience at the moment, and Dawn was in rare form. No matter how Candace tried to compete, even in their adolescence, she would never be five feet, nine inches, that thin, or that brunette.

They met on the veranda near the open French doors which exposed the polished baby grand piano in the parlor. Dawn greeted Candace with an elaborate display of customary

European-style pecks on each cheek, making every effort not to smudge lipstick, preceded by a delicate don't-wrinkle-me hug.

"CJ sweetie, I hope I'm not late." She gushed. "The congressman had some last-minute details to run through. I can't believe we're literally hours away from the fund raiser, and Ronnie wants to change the seating arrangements."

"It happens," Candace assured her.

"Shit happens? Did I hear you correctly, CJ? Shit happens? Well, not to me, not on *my* watch." Dawn raised her voice an octave to make her point. It was likely the governor could have heard her statement from his office down the street.

"It will be fine Dawn. Things like this happen all the time." A small sigh accompanied her clarification. "I just need your table numbers and seating arrangements by 5 p.m. tomorrow."

"Okay, whatever you say."

Dawn was adept at staying consistently in the spotlight and bringing her clients right along with her. The client she off-handedly referred to as Ronnie was Congressman Ronald Tethermeyer, her recent and most prestigious catch, both personally and professionally. He was every woman's dream; tall, dark, handsome and single, with eyes on the White House. Ronnie was of Mexican descent with skin that stayed tan in all seasons, which was easy in a city claiming over 300 days of sunshine a year. His Mexican-American heritage would give him a good chance of winning his bid for a second term, a fact Dawn was paid to focus on.

Another subject Dawn seemed intent on was Uncle Dan. "So, what's the lowdown on your uncle? Was it an accident? Do the cops have any idea yet?"

"Not entirely sure, but the Sheriff and I are pretty convinced he didn't just fall."

"Really? Do you think he'll make it?"

Candace's mood turned grim. "Oh God, Dawn. I can't imagine him not making it. We're waiting for him to wake up anytime. I don't know how to tell him about Merlin though."

"What about Merlin?"

"He's dead. Didn't I tell you?"

Dawn was visibly shaken. "He's what?"

"He died the morning after I found Uncle Dan. Evidently, he was poisoned–both dogs were. The vet said it was Zoloft, the prescription given to people with depression. Uncle Dan wasn't taking it, so I *know* something suspicious happened to Uncle," Candace stated adamantly. "Why else would someone poison his dogs?

"Damn, girlfriend. That's really strange."

"I know."

A pregnant pause ensued.

"Well, let's take one last look at the menu." Dawn changed the subject. "I have my copy right here but it's a little late to change something. Anton will have my head."

"Well, you already have his heart." Dawn commented. "I just need to make sure everything is going to be perfect."

Dismissing her snark, Candace laughed. "I can imagine. The guest list looks like a Who's Who of Denver."

The congressman had selected a popular presentation whereby clusters of hors d'oeuvres would be displayed on metal, glass or porcelain trays and served to guests from waiters carrying them throughout the room. For this party they'd be serving signature selections of veal parmesan sliders, goat cheese wontons with Chipotle caramel dipping sauce, tenderloin lollipops wrapped in bacon and mahi-mahi skewers coated with wasabi sesame seeds. The dinner, a Colorado inspired surf and turf, was a selection of seared mint and rosemary lamb loin, poached crabmeat and asparagus spears drenched in Béarnaise sauce. This would be served alongside Grand Marnier smashed sweet potatoes, creamed corn soufflé and Candace's signature popovers which Dan, and half of Denver, labeled as legendary.

Dawn happily awarded approval of the menu with no alterations but not without asking a dozen or so questions. Unlike

Candace, Dawn was not as informed or knowledgeable about formalities. The daughter of a mathematical genius and stock market tycoon who parlayed his way from the college classroom to the board room knew far more about pizza delivery than elegant table service.

The two spent the next hour traipsing through the three interior levels of the mansion. Nothing much had changed since Candace last worked there. The vast foyer, intimate parlor, and library were dressed with Elizabethan drapes, heavily polished furniture and built-in bookshelves, which were all as regal as ever. The basement contained a defunct bowling alley and space for dancing, and in this case, where photo opportunities with the congressman would be held. They discussed every minute detail of flower and liquor delivery, band placement and the strictly scheduled arrival and departure times of the candidate and his entourage.

The visit was finished in time for Candace to go back to her office, but Dawn quashed that idea. "You've been tied up in knots for days. A little break won't hurt. Go home and chill. I'll meet you at my apartment in a few hours."

She exited with the same speed and agility as she had arrived, like the jungle cat she resembled.

CHAPTER 13

C andace made a quick detour to her office. Dawn should have known work would win out. The familiarity of it would be a welcome change relieving the pent-up stress and worry of the past few days. Collapsing in her desk chair for the first time in a week, Candace closed her eyes and took a whiff of what smelled like searing beef. The aroma reminded her she hadn't eaten all day. There must be a tasting scheduled this afternoon.

To Dine For Catering's commissary, kitchen, and offices were situated in one central location, creating ease of operation under one roof. Candace and Anton had purchased the 1950's Tudor style house nestled near the posh Wash Park area of Denver nearly three years ago. The layout and architecture were perfect for their needs and fed the desire they both shared for historical reverence and ambiance. Candace dreamed of an impressive dining room for tastings with an elegant feel that no strip mall or warehouse could offer, and besides, they'd own it. That is, once the mortgage was paid in full, they would.

They decided on a house that needed plenty of work and lots of re-zoning and permitting. Completely gutting and remodeling the kitchen to make it commercial rather than residential. They also built office space in place of bedrooms. Uncle Dan gave Candace the down payment from her trust fund, but both she and Anton ended up investing lots of sweat equity in the place.

"Hi, Boss!" Romaine said. Playfully nicknamed Ro, she was Candace's right hand gal. What were the odds that the best catering office manager around would be named after a head of lettuce? Ro was Pennsylvania Dutch and a very generous woman in both physical size and heart, a welcome tower of strength wrapped in an apron and was every bit the comforting, confident force Candace needed.

Ro greeted Candace with a venti-sized Starbuck chai latte in hand. She rushed around the side of the desk so that Candace would keep seated, placed the cup on the desk, then and threw her arms around her. "When Anton said you'd be in, I couldn't believe it, but I told myself if anybody would put the job first, it would be you."

"Well, the show must go on and my uncle would be the first person to send me here. The customer is always first, Ro." Candace drew in a big breath of resignation and savored the chai's spicy aroma and creamy taste. "Thanks for this."

"Do we have anybody in house today?" Candace queried.

"Ms. McMahon and her mom are in the selection room. I can handle them, and then we're clear until the tasting at six. I think Cameron is doing it unless Anton makes it in."

"Where's Anton?"

Ro took a sip of her own Starbucks. "Shopping. We need fresh greens for tomorrow."

"Oh, swell. You know how he hates to shop." Candace giggled at the thought.

"I told him I'd go, but he insisted. I don't need to tell you how particular he is."

Candace realized how hungry she was. "That's fine. Do you think the guys could scare up something for me to eat?"

"Sure thing. I think I saw Cameron making some bruschetta."

Candace took a couple more sips of tea and stood up slowly. "Perfect. I'll come in and say hello to the McMahon's, then work on some room layouts and packing lists. If you can look them over, it would be helpful. I'm not thinking as clearly as usual."

"I'd be happy to," Ro said smiling, "There were a couple of calls you might want to return. An attorney named Mr. Long called about an hour ago."

"Harry or Tripp?"

"Oh, he didn't say, but he left a number." Ro followed Candace into the parlor. The front room of the house had been turned into an area where clients viewed and selected dishes, crystal, silver, linens, and colors to be used on their tables and chairs.

Beyond the front room and through sliding pocket doors was a formal sample of a typical event venue with round dining tables and rectangular buffets dressed in usual party fashion. On the other side of the center hallway in the middle of the dining room stood a highly polished cherry wood table and a matching china cabinet filled with crystal goblets and serving pieces once owned by Candace's mother. An impressive wine rack and a marble fireplace were at one end. It was the perfect location for tastings.

The two large bedrooms toward the back of the first floor were taken up by Anton and Candace's offices with Ro's desk just outside their doors. Romaine spent lots of time in the kitchen as well. There didn't seem to be an employee in the company who wasn't passionate about food, whether working to prepare it, serving it, or eating it.

"Mrs. McMahon and Suzanne, how are you today?" Candace graciously greeted the bride and her mother. Her posture erect with her hand outstretched, she pulled them both in for a warm hug. "I can't wait to see your final selections."

The bride and her mother basked in the attention, knowing nothing of Uncle Dan's plight, which was refreshing for Candace.

She sat and nodded approval as Ro took charge and paraded the tablecloth colors and china choices before them.

This was good. Candace had been overwhelmed by Uncle's condition and treatment. Preparing for upcoming nuptials was always uplifting and just being in the room with the betrothed gave her renewed vigor. When the appropriate lull in the conversation came, Ro politely shooed Candace back to work.

Literally her home away from home, her renovated bedroom office was clad in hues of hunter green and raspberry. A taffeta covered couch sat against one wall with a large framed mirror above it, and a Queen Anne writing desk was placed dead center in the room. A built-in bookcase displayed mementos and pictures of dozens of past events featuring Candace and many recognizable faces in Denver society. High-back chairs in green and raspberry plaid with touches of gold were placed before the desk with pillows of the same fabric tossed on the raspberry couch. The room was as bright and colorful as its occupant, although Candace thought it strange that several of the pillows were askew.

An antique coffee table with claw feet held a stunning dried flower arrangement and a spray of bridal magazines for guests to peruse. On the corner of her desk was her pride and joy, an authentic Tiffany lamp with stained glass hues that matched the fabrics. Paintings on the walls were eclectic in taste. Impressionist landscapes and female portraits in bold shades of pinks, greens and yellows framed in antiqued gold. She loved the room and how it made her feel, both pretty and proud, and safe.

On top of the desk was a Waterford crystal candy dish and vase, both gifts from her uncle. Beside them were a crystal paper weight and a marble replica of Thomas Jefferson's favorite piece of architecture, the obelisk, a gift from Anton who loved history as much, or more than, she did. She was surprised to see the vase filled with fresh cut flowers.

Anton must have gotten them this morning. He always made

sure it was full. He was such a dear. She bet he had someone come in and clean while she was gone. Candace rearranged some of the misplaced items on the desktop and buried her nose in the blooms to smell their fragrance.

Checking her computer calendar for the next dated event, Candace was sufficiently relieved. The Alexander-Carver wedding reception at Lionsgate Event Center was up next. The management at the site were responsible for all table set up, dishes, and glasses. The job would be a slam dunk. Floral arrangements would be set by the venue as would the tablecloths, chair covers and napkins. This particular venue was an old dairy farm gatehouse which now possessed every accoutrement a wedding party could possibly desire. In addition to a groom's suite upstairs, there was a bridal bedroom with a four-poster bed, mirrored antique dressing table and elegantly appointed chaises for the attendants to relax on before making their grand entrance. A five-thousand-square-foot ballroom was adorned with a magnificent wood floor throughout, crystal chandeliers and stained-glass windows. Down a few steps, an enclosed sunroom created the perfect setting for a double-sided buffet. There was little to do to make this a visual success.

Candace clicked the mouse to open the file and review the menu. Just as she began to focus, the door swung open to reveal a very serious young man dressed in a spotless white chef's jacket and pressed black pants carrying a tray full of appetizers. As usual, Cameron was very GQ in appearance with the exception of black Crocs dirtied with mud. It was clear he had ridden his bike to work again from Cook Street, the local culinary school where he had begun formal training.

"CJ, I've been worried sick about you, and Anton's been a mess," he said as he set down the tray and placed the dishes in front of Candace. "But, don't tell him I said so."

"Oh, Cammie," Candace said the nickname only she dared use. "You're a sight for sore eyes!" She turned her face upward for the kiss she knew would be planted on her cheek. "Has he really been a mess?"

"He sure has but tries like hell not to show it. I'm so glad you're here." His hug was warm and sincere. Cameron was a gracious and eloquent young man, worldly beyond his years, and Candace had recognized his potential long ago. Shy and understated, his chocolate-colored curls fell softly around his eyes, giving him a tender almost innocent expression, but the twinkle they possessed and the wink he often used told another tale.

"How's your uncle doing? I was so sorry to hear about his condition." His voice was deep with a soft and gentle tone. He walked behind her chair, squeezed and kneaded her shoulders like pastry, which made it difficult to decide if she should sink back and enjoy or eat some morsels from the dish in front of her.

"He's still in a coma, Cammie. I just can't believe it. The police don't have any evidence, and I don't know what to think." She shook her head. "At first, like everyone else, I thought it was an attempted robbery, but now they say nothing was taken or disturbed except for some boxes of papers."

"Wow. What do the doctors say about his recovery?" It was just like Cameron to show he was far more concerned for her uncle than about the money or other things.

"It's a wait-and-see game. They're saying time will tell, but I need him to wake up. He's got to have some recollection of what happened, and then maybe I can get the police moving. I don't care what they say, I think it was deliberate." She went on to tell him about Merlin and the drugging of both dogs.

"Who would wanna hurt a guy and his dogs? He's like Robin Hood. Please let me know when Bri and I can go see him. We're free after this weekend, and we're always here for you, lady." Cameron and his girlfriend Brianna had been dating for several years and became engaged while working at To Dine For Catering. Their plan was to open their own restaurant one day. He leaned over kissing the top of his mentor's head.

Candace choked up and squeezed her eyes shut to block the tears that unexpectedly accompanied his display of affection. She cleared her throat. "I will, and I know you are. Let's see if we can concentrate on work. Help me focus, please. We still need to get everything ordered for this weekend and the congressman's dinner on Thursday."

"You got it," he said, pulling up a chair to the desk. "Hey, you wanna smoke a bowl before we do? It'll help you relax." Cameron, ever the equalizer and keeper of the company weed supply.

Candace shook her head. "Not now. I need to focus. I really need you and Ro to take point on helping Anton now. Did I tell you my friend Dawn was running that one?"

"Yeah. Anton told me she was doing the promotional work. How'd she get mixed up with a congressman? Is he married?" Cameron smiled and winked that wink.

"Now, Cammie, give the girl a break." Candace knew he was referring to the fact that Dawn was pretty well known around town, showing up to all the hot spots on the arm of every eligible, and not so eligible, man in Denver.

"Okay, okay." He laughed as Ro came in.

"What's going on, Cam?" Ro asked.

"Just talking about The Dawn, and don't call me that!" He jumped up, flinging his arm around Ro's neck, holding her in a brotherly headlock.

"Oh, so you heard about her shindig with the congressman?" Ro said matter-of-factly.

Cam frowned. "Yep, I guess she'll be bossing us all around without CJ there."

Dawn had had more than her share of bad luck or Karma, as she would call it. Candace always defended the underdog. "All right you two, that's enough. I know she can be difficult, but she's had it tough."

"Maybe I'll just get her high, and she'll chill out a bit," said Cam."

96

Shaking her head, Candace remembered the circumstances surrounding the death of Dawn's father when she was only fourteen. Without the counseling and structure that Candace had been fortunate to have, it was really no wonder she'd ended up getting arrested for shoplifting by the time she was sixteen. No amount of money could keep her out of age appropriate incarceration and drug rehab. Further assaults to her record were all expunged by age eighteen, but she continued to live life on the edge.

It wasn't until her mother was diagnosed with cancer that Dawn began to repair their estrangement. They took a trip to Japan where Dawn learned about the culture. It was their physically demanding exercise regimes she credited for getting her head on straight. Upon returning to the States, Dawn took classes at a top Manhattan advertising and design firm and lived with her mom in Connecticut. When Marjorie entered remission, Dawn ended up in Denver to remain close to memories of her father and to start her own PR firm with his former list of extensive contacts.

"She's a real piece of work. You know Bri hates her," he said it as if the fact his girlfriend disapproval was huge. It was common knowledge that Brianna was a sweetheart and loved everyone.

"She came down to the hospital in the middle of the night." Candace countered, not quite sure why Dawn had that effect on people.

Cam scoffed. "Seriously? Did she want to pick up a doctor or something?"

"Probably a plastic surgeon." Ro snickered and freed herself by poking Cam in the ribs, and then said, "Sorry."

"Cut her some slack, guys. My uncle and I have known her since we were kids." Candace continued. "Come on, let's put our heads in some menus."

Candace ignored the fact that Ro flashed Cameron a knowing look and settled into ordering inventory for the upcoming wedding. The menus were broken down and each item added to a purveyor list. Pickups and deliveries were scheduled and two hours later the food for the weekend was set. Ro would double-check deliveries the morning of the event, and Cam would make sure all prepped items arrived in proper quantities and in good condition.

"Anton won't ask for an extra pair of hands, but at least he'll have this part covered," she said.

The bridal menu consisted of a cocktail station with assorted fresh fruits and imported cheeses cascading from the base of a three-foot-tall pineapple palm tree as the centerpiece for the buffet. Once there, hours of work went into the creation of the tree itself with real palm fronds purchased from the local florist that would rise out of the top. Fussing with the tree was Cameron's department. Deferring to the bride's personal taste, the cheese board was comprised of Saga Bleu and smoked Gouda with flatbreads and poppy seed crackers.

The wedding also called for a seafood display in a round copper tub, loaded with ice and hundreds of jumbo Rooibos-tea-marinated shrimp, accompanied by several sauces and a marble slab presentation of roasted vegetables, along with Italian sausage slices and toasted Crostini rounds brushed with seasoned olive oil.

That was one of Uncle Dan's favorites. Candace sighed. Nothing in her life would ever be the same without him. She picked up the phone to call the hospital, and as she did, a voice on the other end said, "Hello...Hello?"

"Oh, hi, Dawn, I was just calling out. You must be psychic," Candace said.

"I tried you on your cell but got the voicemail. I had a feeling you went to work anyway. Can't you ever just relax?" Dawn, ever the critic. "Do you still want to catch dinner or are you going to squirm out of our plans?"

"I can. I'm not squirming out of anything, but I thought you'd end up doing something with the congressman tonight."

"No, he'll be in Washington until the event. He's a busy guy, and I'm trying really hard not to seem desperate."

Candace was amused for the first time in days. "You, desperate? Hardly."

"You don't know the half of it. Besides, it's a lot harder trying not to seem desperate than it is actually being desperate, if you get my drift. Why don't you ask the Russian hunk to join us? I'm sure he'd love to."

"What? You're a crazy woman, and yes, I'll ask him. Thanks."

Dawn asked, "Okay, how about we meet at my place and go together?"

"We can try the new Cuban restaurant. I could go for some really good *Ropa Vieja*." Candace remembered that culinary street treat from south Miami. People came to Denver and tried to duplicate it but never really succeeded. She suspected the ocean air and tropically grown plantains were the secret to the Cuban flavor.

"Yes! And we'll get some rice and black beans."

Candace confirmed. "Okay, I'll see you around seven?"

Dawn chuckled. "You mean seven o'clock for real or seven Cuban time?"

"I mean seven, Anton time. You know how punctual *he* is! I've got to finish up here. See you later."

"Okay, don't work too hard." With that, Dawn hung up.

Candace shook her head. The two of them couldn't be more different. Dawn was a party animal while Candace would rather stay home, whip up something to eat and curl up with a good book. She already knew Dawn would drag her from club to club after dinner and was ashamed to admit she'd let it happen.

CHAPTER 14

Candace's conversation with Tripp's father, Harry Long was an unpleasant. He quickly verified that no heroic measures of any kind would be used to save her uncle and confirmed a will had been in place for years. However, he also inferred that not just Candace and Jesse were within its provisions. Preserving the attorney-client privilege, he couldn't say much more. He did insist all legal avenues be exhausted to clear up the matter of whether it was an accident or an attack. He told her he'd leave the paperwork at the office with Tripp and hoped to see Dan at the hospital on Saturday. He delivered instructions to call with any change in his condition.

Still uncomfortable about not being able to coerce details from the elder Long, Candace ended the conversation. Someone else was in Uncle's will. She looked down at her skirt which was wrinkled from sitting in the car and behind her desk all day. She strode over to the walk-in closet and selected a nice pair of jeans. She wondered if Tripp could give her more information. Seeing him tomorrow was definitely necessary even though it would surely open a can of worms and release countless feelings.

Her five-piece office bathroom was finished in ivory marble

tile with bamboo accents. It had been one real benefit of their refurbish. When the staff prepped for parties, Candace could slip away, slide into the tub, refresh, and dress before a big night while still being handy. The jetted bathtub and spa were her favorite part of the house, second only to the kitchen.

Sliding into tight blue jeans, Colorado's design equivalent to a little black dress, and a white tank top sequined with a single rose entwined in thorny branches, she tossed her head and brushed her locks forward to smooth out some of the natural curl. She shook her head and ran her fingers through her hair.

That was better. She nodded her approval in the mirror. However, she still looked sleep deprived. She grabbed a short dark-green suede jacket that matched some of stem work on the top and went down the hall to Anton's office. She loved how closely they worked, their offices and their growing success. Up until this week everything had been as she hoped and planned it would. Now life was marching on as usual except for the fact Uncle Dan wasn't awake.

Anton was sitting at his all-glass desk playing chess on the computer. The chrome legs and cross supports to his workspace looked very modern. She noticed he too, had changed. He wore an expensive pair of pleated black slacks, impeccably tailored with a skinny snakeskin belt which peeked under the loosely tucked gray-blue silk shirt. When he turned to greet her, his smoky eyes reflected that color, set off by his thick black lashes.

"Do we have to go?" Anton pleaded. "Let's stay here. I'll make you dinner."

She sat on the couch and dug in her purse for makeup. "I want to go. You don't have to go with us."

"I want to go, but with you, only with you," he said quietly.

"I know, but can't you just tolerate her tonight...for me?" Her voice raised pleadingly. "My schedule is so limited right now."

Anton sighed.

His office definitely reflected his personal taste. Nature filled the room. A black leather sectional with cream-colored throw pillows embroidered with black bears and moose heads sat haphazardly in opposing corners. Hunter green was the color of choice and large potted ornamental evergreens rose from the corners of the room. A small elk chandelier Uncle Dan had given him hung over one end table, and an animal skin area rug finished the overall woodland theme.

His bookcases were overflowing with books, Indian artifacts, and pottery. Most of the pieces were from trips he had taken either hiking or canoeing on the Arkansas River. Pictures of deer, buffalo and elk in their natural habitat hung on the walls, most taken in the snow. Anton was just as passionate about snow as he was about food and could be found on the slopes snowboarding and skiing when he wasn't cooking.

"Please just go with us."

Anton conceded. "Okay, but only for you, my кукла."

"Good." She was relieved to have his company, and put her mind to her uncle. "I called the hospital again. They told me his blood work looks good, and his oxygen level is rising."

The only true measure of how she was doing at the moment was through the condition of her uncle.

"I called as well. They said no change, which is what they always tell me," Anton added, shutting off his computer.

She finished putting on her face, a term her mother would use, and snapped her compact mirror shut. "I know. I hate that. I've told them they can tell you anything."

"He's going to be fine, I'm sure. And when they find out who did this, I'm going hunting, for real. In the meantime, I'm very much a hungry bear, so we better get going, or I might eat your little friend for dinner." He got up and crossed the room with his brow furrowed.

Candace winked and gave him a big smile. "She'd probably love being devoured by you."

"Ha, ha, very funny." He extended his arm and pulled her up from the couch into a great big hug.

Candace laughed for the first time in days. "I saw her at the site visit today. She said she came by and borrowed the dress for the party."

"Ah, yes she did. What else did she say?" He looked into her face and planted a very soft and tender peck on her newly pink nose.

"Nothing much. Almost changed the menu but didn't."

"Good," Anton let out a breath and wrapped an arm around her waist. They strolled out to the car, giggling as if it were any other evening.

CHAPTER 15

As Anton circled the block, Candace waited for Dawn in her apartment, studying an array of silver and crystal picture frames atop the piano. The black baby grand was the focal point in a loft decorated stark white with splashes of neon yellow. The only exception was the addition of hot-pink faux zebra print on her dining chairs and throw pillows tossed on the white leather sectional.

A lemon-tipped white shag rug sprawled across the ebony laminate floor. Black and white prints of Marilyn Monroe, Elvis Presley and the 1950's Rat Pack framed in fluorescent-yellow lacquer hung on the exterior walls. The room was dimly lit with the exception of the posters and other art showcased by pinpoint spotlights suspended from ceiling rafters. Uncle Dan teased that the art deco influenced space had some "early boudoir" thrown in for good measure. Candace didn't care much for it, but it oddly suited Dawn.

"Are you almost ready? Anton's in the car downstairs." she called.

"Coming!" Dawn answered from the bedroom.

"Hurry up."

A single black and white snapshot, protected under glass like a treasured museum artifact, caught Candace's attention. It was a photo of Dawn's father, Eric, and the Kane boys back in the day. They had been captured in time, celebrating a big win at a senior football game. The three posed at the edge of the stadium bleachers, Eric in his lettered sweater flanked by Brad and Dan in their uniforms and helmets with their arms slung over Eric's shoulders. Candace's dad and uncle sported toothy grins like a pair of bulldog bookends. It was hard to believe two of these men were already gone, and now, Uncle Dan was clinging to life.

Eric Ehrlickson had been a friend of the Kane family since Candace's father and uncle moved to South Florida and began attending the same high school. For three years they ran with the same group of friends and spent nearly all of their spare time at Miami Beach. For all of their closeness, Eric was the antithesis of the brothers. He was passionate about track, not football and a devotee of chess club rather than rubbing elbows with the after-school soda fountain crowd. He was built like a swimmer—long and lean with toned muscles and a rippled six-pack, unlike the pair of gorillas. Also by contrast, getting into an Ivy League college was a slam dunk for Eric, if not from his own grade point average then through his family's connections, where Dan and Brad were both expected to deliver on a scholarship.

"Do you think our dads and Uncle Dan had any idea what they'd end up doing back then and how far they'd go?" Candace called out to Dawn. She struggled to ask her if she knew about the letters.

"Oh, I don't think so. I remember Dad telling me it was your dad and uncle's pet project to rescue him after my grandmother died in their senior year." Dawn now stood in the doorway gazing at the picture, too. "He said they both really showed him a good time. If it wasn't for their antics, he didn't know if he would have pulled through."

"Yeah, they knew what it felt like to lose a parent. I hear they tried really hard to keep his mind off it and to help him graduate." Candace thought about her own struggle and physically shuddered at the possibly of losing her uncle. "You about ready?"

Candace was always a bit jealous of Dawn's figure and her ability to slip on anything and have it fit just right. Tonight, it was jeans with a cream-colored silk blouse, a brown leather jacket and saddle color boots. Very Denver.

"Yes, be right there. The stories I heard were colorful, I'll give 'em that," Dawn commented over her shoulder as she turned back to her bedroom. "Dad said every weekend the three of them hung out like the Musketeers, cruised the beach, and slayed the hearts of eligible young ladies, but I'm not really sure who helped who. It's creepy, don't ya think? I mean, first your dad and uncle lost their father so young, and my grandmother died when my dad was in high school, then you were orphaned at thirteen the same year my dad croaked. I'd say we're effin' cursed."

"Dawn!" Candace said in an alarmed and chastising tone. She never could support her friend's coarse use of the vernacular nor her perception on life. Candace really wanted to say how creepy it was about Uncle Dan and Dawn's mom but thought better of it.

"You really need to chill," she said, finally ready and made her way toward Candace.

"You know, your dad really was good looking," Candace observed, changing the topic. "Was he always so serious? I don't remember him like that."

"Pretty much," Dawn said thoughtfully. "Good old Dad, he was all about business."

Maybe if he wasn't, Aunt Marj would have been happier. Candace was certain of one thing. Uncle Dan's role of big brother to both Brad and Eric. He challenged them in everything—sports, grades, and certainly in business over the years. They competed in any arena where one could keep score. After graduation, Eric entered a corporate position while Brad opened his clothing manufacturing business with Cynthia, but Dan bested them both. Surprisingly, Eric and Brad succeeded where Dan missed out entirely—in the affairs of the heart. Unlike Uncle Dan, the younger men met their wives within months of each other and were married until their deaths. Of course, now she knew all was not as it seemed.

"They weren't much older than you and I are now when they were in the thick of it all," Candace said loudly enough to be heard. "Of course, your dad had the investment capital, but he and Uncle Dan sure were powerhouses."

"Mmhmm, I remember your uncle's meteoric rise from floor trader to investment manager, then opening that huge brokerage office here in Denver." Dawn bent over a mirrored frame to catch her reflection and twisted her lip gloss cover to apply it heavily. "Always wondered what he had to do to get there."

"What do you mean?" Candace asked.

"Dunno, just sayin'." Dawn gathered her bag and a scarf from the foyer closet and experimented with different looks.

As far as Candace knew, Uncle Dan's sharp eye for growth potential and keen business sense made him the imposing figure he became on Wall Street, nothing more, nothing less. She had to hold her breath to refrain from asking Dawn what she was inferring by that comment.

Instead she asked, "Isn't this picture in front of the Brown Palace Hotel the time your dad and mom visited us and almost moved your family to Colorado?"

Candace touched another framed memory.

Dawn was not only reflective but Candace noticed a glint in her eye and she sounded surprisingly astute about it all. "Yup, things were sure different back then, Dad always said the 80's were all about growth, expansion and high interest rates. Everything they touched seemed to turn to gold."

"Whoa! Listen to you. I always wondered why you didn't

follow in your father's footsteps. By now I bet you'd have a corporate jet, penthouse offices in New York and Boston and never look back."

"What's that old saying? When I got around to wanting what he had, what he had wasn't worth wanting? After Dad was gone, Mom thought about living in Denver. Not exactly the stock market capital of the world." Dawn sounded contrite. "I'll always remember our dads joking about the fact Denver was nothing more than a small horse-trading town pretending to be a big metropolis. Besides, after your father died, your uncle had no use for business and he was the one who knew it all."

Dawn was correct about her take on the financial climate back then, and it was Dan who most enjoyed predicting which companies were ripe for the takeover picking. Eric and his wealthy friends, devoted movers and shakers, all loved to follow Uncle Dan's particular style of harvesting and snatching profits. It was common knowledge Eric not only loved the kinship but also the money and his chance to become a boardroom buddy of Dan's.

Once Candace's parents were killed, her uncle's focus turned to condensing his personal portfolio, liquidating his brother's holdings, and trying his hand at surrogate parenting. He relinquished all client account management and the hands-on nurturing of companies to the New York office executive VP's and senior analysts. It was clear Dawn felt Uncle Dan left her dad stranded in a sea of investment waters that turned choppy as the 90's emerged and, according to the letters in the attic, stranded without the love of his wife. Candace wondered if Dawn felt Dan was responsible for her father's suicide. Maybe Dawn confronted him about the letters. Maybe she had been the one who had attacked him. Candace quickly dismissed the thought.

"Hey, are you ready to blow this pop stand? I thought we'd go to some clubs in Lo-Do. I know how much you *love* it there." Dawn grinned and winked while marching out the door. Denver's popular lower downtown entertainment district was where anyone who was anyone spent evenings networking, dating, or in Dawn's case, usually carousing.

I knew it. Candace frowned. Anton would certainly hate parading around town while Dawn was making connections.

CHAPTER 16

Candace knew all too well that Dawn had been drinking since she was knee-high to a grasshopper and could really hold her liquor. It didn't surprise her when following an incredible Cuban meal, Dawn convinced them both to join her for a drink. One great aspect of Denver was its abundant number of bars per square block. Cowboys with wide brims and corporate types with ties were happy to cough up whatever funds were necessary to keep girls, like Dawn placated and dancing.

Although Candace knew this was not a choice spot in Anton's mind, when Dawn offered to spring for the drinks, she watched as Anton acquiesced and imbibed. He ordered Russian vodka, neat, tossed it back then promptly excused himself feigning exhaustion. Against his upbringing but well deserved, he left the tab for Dawn.

Very little time passed before Candace elected to move them away from the bar into a booth, but Dawn would have no part in it. Coveting their time alone, drinking shooters while Candace sipped wine, Dawn reminisced. "You know, my dad was on top for so many years," she spoke, looking into a shooter. "They didn't call him "The Brick" for nothing."

"I haven't heard you talk about your dad for a long time. I can't believe you remembered his old nickname."

Their conversation in the apartment earlier must have touched a nerve.

Dawn didn't hesitate to down that shot and order another. "If it wasn't for Black Monday in 1987, life would have been so different."

"Remember that day we found out about Dad?" Dawn squeezed Candace's arm so hard red fingerprints were left on it.

Candace could see this wasn't heading to a good place and was a bit uncomfortable with the topic herself. "You know, maybe we should get you home."

"That fall after the car accident at the ranch—remember?" Dawn asked slurring her words.

"Yes, I remember." That day had been the first time Candace was sure Dawn really understood how she felt.

Candace's psychiatric treatment in Florida ended in late summer after plans for her to attend boarding school were thwarted by her serious bout with depression. She and Uncle Dan were taking a much-needed vacation on the newly baptized 'Double K' as fall kicked in. It seemed fitting to recognize their newly formed "family" in this way, and Dawn had joined them. Most of the conversations centered on where Candace would now attend and finish high school. They had pretty much decided she would give the school a try if Dawn would go with her. It seemed like a great solution. It was agreed that Uncle Dan would hire a tutor to work with both girls over the holidays to get them ready.

Dan accepted a call one afternoon that changed their well laid plans. He was informed Dawn's father had ended his life the prior evening with a single gunshot to the head. As her uncle shared in the eulogy, he gave days later, he had lost his best friend. There would be no more daily phone calls, no guidance requests, no more raucous parties, off color jokes or juicy stories to share. He would be sorely missed.

The immediate sensory blackout was palpable. Dan lost a partner, and Dawn's world was altered as if her own father had driven off a cliff.

"That bitch!" Dawn flipped another shooter into her mouth.

Candace suspected she knew the bitch Dawn was referring to.

She clearly remembered the media took hold of the story with a vengeance. Eric "The Brick" Ehrlickson had invested his substantial holdings with Dan's firm in Colorado. As the markets began to slide along with many stock offerings, adjustments were made by those tracking the market closely with the exception of one of Dan's VP's, Ms. Pamela Lloyd-Everett.

Uncle Dan had described his VP several times, each time adding more of her snake-like features. Candace pictured a tall, seductive blonde fresh out of Stanford. A threat to all masculinity, she stood taller than most when she wore spiked heels with her designer wool suits and open-necked pastel silk blouses. Appropriate below the knee pencil skirts, and seamed stockings provided an unmistakable accent to the back of her slender calves. Dan described her as smooth as the serpent in the Garden of Eden, but their garden was bank and brokerage house conference rooms. She slithered deeper into Dan's business once he was otherwise occupied by the loss of his brother and sister-in-law and parenting his new ward.

Dan tracked little of the day-to-day operation back then. The bottom line was Pamela used her slimy ways to infiltrate and boast impressive earnings on the back of Dan's best friend's portfolio. According to Uncle Eric, Pamela painted a powerful picture for clients eager to turn a profit. Stocks and bonds held closely by baby-boomers were, in her opinion, on par with purchasing a family station wagon. These investments were deemed staid and boring when any man's real desire was to take a spin in a late model sports car. She spent her time orchestrating the liquidation of their assets while advising them to buy targeted investments that by her definition was more like "speeding toward wealth with the top down" helping her own commissions race everyone else's to the finish line.

Accusations were widespread in the investment community and shared around the dinner table. It would have all but ruined Uncle Dan had charges not been filed against Lloyd-Everett and Pamela, summarily fired. Her exit from the firm did little to heal the devastation or comfort friends of Eric when he shot himself a week later, the newspapers reported. Stories that made Dawn hate her viciously.

Dan tried to rectify the hole in all their lives. Having sold or protected his own investments, he saw to it the girls spent quality time with him on all school vacations and provided trips abroad, lessons in scuba diving and horseback riding, spa weekends and concert excursions complete with backstage passes and limousine escorts. He sent both young ladies on a twenty-one-day cruise of the Greek Isles for a graduation present, and if that wasn't enough, they celebrated their eighteenth birthdays on a joint trip to Paris. It was then Uncle told Candace, if money could not buy happiness, it certainly helped to see the girls' smile after years of tears and misery.

Candace was desperate to get Dawn off this depressing roller coaster of memories. "Dawn, I've found it's best if we don't dwell on all of it. It's in the past."

"Sometimes the past is the only place I feel accepted or comfortable, Miss Candy Kane." Dawn snorted.

Candace cringed. "Well, I try really hard to concentrate on the happier times. Do you remember all those trips we took with your mom to Manhattan for fashion week? What did she used to call them—fashion junkets? I swear she would have flown us halfway around the world trying to be a replacement for my mother. She never could tolerate designers west of the Mississippi." Candace knew instinctively if her own mom were still in her life, she would have been just as involved in fashion week and designer collections.

"Well aren't you a Pollyanna? My mom always did treat you like royalty. What the hell was so great about you? You have no idea what it was like to be me." Dawn swilled back another shot and splayed across the bar.

Candace motioned for the bartender placing her index finger on one side of her neck making a slow movement across, as if to slit her throat, signifying the end of drink service. She really didn't know what to say at this juncture and had too much on her own mind. It was better to just take Dawn home and end the night. She certainly wouldn't want to remind her of any further reason to despair. Though Candace lost both parents when she was young, it was obvious Dawn was the one who felt more isolated and alone. It was true, Candace's parents died in an accident, not at their own hand. Who knew how Eric's unhappiness had affected Dawn? Clearly, Aunt Marj had been unhappy as well.

Candace removed Dawn's heels and a scarf from around her neck as she practically poured her into her bed. She hoped Dawn didn't throw up on her Gucci blouse. Candace rustled through Dawn's drawers for pajamas. She settled on an oversized Victoria Secret sleep shirt and slipped it on so she could crash on the couch while Dawn slept it off. She padded across the hardwood floor into the kitchen to grab a snack of cheese and crackers and a glass of Sprite, then called voicemail.

Tripp had called confirming her visit to his dad's office tomorrow. Anton checked in more than once, concerned with her whereabouts, and Sheriff Sam called to ask for contact info on Anton and Dawn. Why on earth would he want to talk to either of them?

Then, Jesse had left the oddest message around nine pm. "I hope you're coming back tonight. The sheriff came by to question me, and I don't know what to do. I will be at the ranch later. Please come home by morning."

It was too late to return the call, but her plan was to leave first thing in the morning. What did Sam want with Jesse? He had questioned *her?*

A quick call to the nurse's station revealed no change in Uncle Dan's condition.

Sleep would be an elusive commodity tonight.

CHAPTER 17

The early morning sun reflected from the floor-to-ceiling wall mirror into Candace's eyes. A mile closer to the big ball of fire than most places in the country, it seemed to shine on Denver for the majority of every day, summer, winter, spring or fall. She stretched and grimaced against the pain in her neck and shoulders. Expensive skinny leather couches were built for design, not comfort, and left little to be desired for sleeping. Thankfully, not a peep came from Dawn's bedroom all night. Candace hoped that meant Dawn had gotten some uninterrupted sleep. The fundraiser was less than twelve hours away, and the last thing she needed was a hung-over, cranky hostess.

She had a full day ahead. She would get dressed and leave before Dawn woke, head down to Gallegos, confer with the doctors, talk to Sam about the investigation, check in at the ranch, get to Harry Long's office, grab the paperwork, interrogate Tripp, and be back by four o'clock for the event. She didn't need to wear anything fancy and had two or three chef coats and a few after party dresses in the closet at the office.

Candace took a shower, tried to find an acceptable fragrance of perfume and slipped into a simple black shirt to freshen her pair of straight leg jeans. Her shoes from last night would have to suffice since Dawn's feet had always been humongous. Her strappy high-heeled sandals weren't made for comfort, but luckily she kept a change of boots at the ranch.

A piece of dry toast and a small glass of orange juice was all the breakfast the kitchen was equipped to provide. Assuming that Dawn would hardly be in the mood to eat for several hours, if at all today, she wiped crumbs from the counter, rinsed out the glass, and took off.

"You've got to be kidding me!" Candace exploded into her cell on the way to Gallegos. Vexed by lack of a decent night's sleep, the last thing she wanted to hear was some stupid assumption from Sheriff Sam as to the identity of her uncle's attacker.

"Look, CJ, we have reason to believe that Pedro Alvarez had a motive for trying to kill your uncle." Sheriff Sam was firm in his resolve. "When you get back to town, please come by the station. We can go over the details."

"I can't come to the station. I need to get to the hospital and back to Denver in time to work an event. I don't have time for this, Sam. Why would Jesse's son Pedro want to kill my uncle?" She was speeding and impatient at the endless expanse of road in front of her.

"It seems he has a long history of jealousy where Jesse and your uncle are concerned. Word around town is he blames your uncle for his parents' divorce and was drinking heavily that night. You told me yourself you couldn't reach Jesse the night of the attack. She admits she was bailing her son out of jail. He'd been arrested for being drunk and disorderly."

No wonder Jesse called her last night.

"I've taken him in for questioning. I spoke with the mother, and she can't alibi him," he continued.

Jessie was likely a wreck. Confronted by the police, Uncle unconscious, and her son a suspect? Candace had to talk to her.

Candace gripped her phone tight. "This is just hogwash. Don't question Pedro without his attorney, Sam. If Jesse doesn't have one, I'll get one. Do you understand?"

"Why would you want to protect someone who almost killed your uncle?"

"Because I'm sure he didn't do it, and I owe it to Jesse to help in whatever way I can. The kid is young and just doesn't get their relationship. Many people have wondered about them over the years, including her own husband, but that doesn't prove anything, and it certainly doesn't mean Pedro would kill over it. Why, after all these years?"

"I'm just telling you what we turned up. I shouldn't even be discussing it with you but he looks good for it, CJ. I'm going to get his DNA to help prove it."

"Don't you dare test his DNA!" Candace just needed some time to talk to Jesse and get a lawyer there. She ended the call abruptly to call the ranch. Getting no response, she called Jesse's cell phone. No answer. Now what?

It was pedal to the metal all the way to Gallegos.

Reaching the hospital a little after eleven, Candace beelined to ICU. Thankfully Sam was otherwise occupied and would not be there to greet her today. It seemed like forever since she'd been in this place, an environment that had been so alien just last week.

Peering through the sliding glass door, Candace saw a woman standing uncomfortably close to Uncle Dan's bedside. She was could have been mistaken for hospital staff, but her snug-fitting, periwinkle business suit was not hospital garb. The smart, peplum waist jacket accentuated her Monroe hips and, towering at over six feet, she was elevated on a pair of hot-pink Steve Madden pumps. A wide brimmed floppy hat of the same garish color concealed all but a few wisps of gray hair at liberty to roam.

"May I help you?" Candace asked curtly.

The woman turned, revealing a broad Aztec-tan framed smile with teeth bearing the resemblance to a chimpanzee. "Candace? It can't be! Just look at you, a ravishing young woman." The older woman gushed as she extended both her arms wide.

Candace was in no mood for games or hugs and kept a safe distance. "Uh, thank you, but who are you?"

"One would hope you'd remember me, dear, but I guess not. I was once engaged to your uncle. My name is Genevieve, Genevieve Morgenstern?" She held out her slender well-manicured hand as her tone elevated into a question.

Candace shook it then compelled herself to withdraw and stop staring. "I, I do remember you. Not clearly, but I've heard stories of you. What brings you here?"

"Your Uncle, of course. Why, I could scarcely stay away knowing his life hung in the balance after everything we meant to each other."

In Candace's opinion, the woman dramatically over pouted her heavily lip-sticked mouth. So, this was the infamous Genevieve. What did he ever see in her? It had been about eighteen years but...really? Makeup born in the 50's, a pinched and turned up nose and that hair. Did they even do that hideous lavender-platinum color anymore?

"Won't you sit down?" Candace motioned to the only chair in the room besides the stiff leather recliner which had become Candace's bed. "The doctors aren't really allowing visitors at this time, just immediate family."

"My dear girl, you really don't remember me, do you? She sat down on the hard surface which didn't seem to agree with her. "You must know your uncle and I were deeply in love. In fact, one might say inseparable. He taught me how to ice skate and ski, both on the water and snow, and how to invest in the stock market. I taught him to speak French, choose proper wine and appreciate the love of a good woman. He just never seemed to get the last part, but then again, I guess I didn't catch on too quickly about stocks either," she said with a hearty laugh, throwing her head back so brusquely, she nearly lost the hat. She grabbed it at the crown and pushed it back down, securing it with a large pearl stick pin.

Candace cringed. "I remember going water skiing with you, my uncle and my parents once or twice and, I *do* remember the day we had to cancel your wedding."

"Yes, well, I was certainly more than just a dalliance. Truth be known, he really swept me off my feet. It was a shame it ended."

"It's really none of my business. I just know how hurt Uncle was at the time."

"I thought we were made for each other, too, but then a heart wants what the heart wants. I fell madly in love with one of his business associates." Genevieve put both of her palms against her lap and faced Candace directly. "Really, what's a girl to do? I *was* just a girl then, you know. Young at heart if not in years. You're a woman now, certainly you understand the pitfalls of romance."

Candace said, "No one understood at the time, I know that." Seriously? This woman swept Uncle off his feet and dropped him like a hot potato. He was devastated and never really got over it according to her Mom. None of us has seen her since, and now she just surfaces? She must be up to something.

"Well, it's all in the past now, isn't it?" Genevieve removed a mirror from her purse and checked her reflection. "So, tell me, dear, there doesn't seem to be anyone else here, is there a Mrs. Kane?"

"No Mrs. Kane. Uncle never settled down. I came to live with him which made dating difficult, I'm sure."

"I wouldn't be hard on yourself, sweetie. Your uncle always adored you. I can't imagine how you two got along after that terrible accident."

"We managed." Candace left it at that.

Genevieve's brows furrowed, giving the appearance of concern. "I did want to come to the funeral and express my sympathies but since the accident wasn't all that long after our breakup, I felt it was better to keep my distance."

"Yes, probably so."

"Do you live here with Dan in New Mexico?"

Candace was tiring of this. "No, I'm a caterer in Denver."

"A caterer? Well, I'll be! That's a pretty big departure from your mama's line of work. She made the loveliest sportswear!"

Dan's nurse entered the room, making the rounds, and levied a look of surprise at the stranger. "The doctor didn't say anything about your uncle having visitors, Ms. Kane."

Candace stood up. "Oh, I know. An old friend of my uncle's stopped by but she was just leaving."

"Well, I suppose doctor's orders and all." Genevieve stood, smoothed her skirt and adjusted her hat. "Candace dear, I do hope you'll clear it with his doctor so that I can come back to visit soon."

"Soon, yes," she agreed but made no mental note to do so.

As Genevieve gathered her purse, she said, "I do want to see him again. I've arranged for a hotel room close by, so you can let me know. By the way, I'm sure someone is looking into it, but did your uncle leave an insurance policy or a will?"

"I, I really don't know." Harry's words echoed in her mind. Could this woman be the "someone else" mentioned in the Will? Candace continued, "In any case, I don't think it's really necessary to concern ourselves with that since he's going to be just fine."

"One never really knows, does one?" The woman placed an unwelcome arm around Candace's shoulder as they walked toward the door. "You might want to scout out his attorney, dear, that dreadfully good-looking wealthy fellow. Harry, oh what was his name? Short or Long something? I'm sure he would know if they're still bosom buddies."

Genevieve squeezed Candace's and gave her a personal calling card and left, parading out with a modelesque stride, her Madden heels clip clopping down the hall.

Candace shook her head in an attempt to throw off the feeling she was just pecked apart by a gaggle of geese. She straightened Uncle's pillow and tucked the edge of his blanket.

"No offense, Uncle, but that woman? What an odd creature. I sure am glad you didn't end up with her," she spoke aloud. "Why on earth would she take an interest in your will? What makes her think she has any connection to you at all? She really is a kook. Anyway, I'm glad I got in touch with your attorney."

Inconsistencies at an all-time high, and nothing in her blood stream but the remnants of her non-breakfast, Candace's head swirled. She sat down in the recliner as thoughts of her uncle's past came rushing back as clearly as if they were yesterday's news cycle. The wedding of the decade in investment circles that was doomed from the moment Genevieve acquired a taste for money and power and coveted both. Candace heard the story more than once about his crushed dreams of a romantic future with Genevieve when she announced a senior business associate would be flying off with her to the couple's pre-booked island honeymoon destination in Dan's stead.

CHAPTER 18

It was just past two o'clock when Candace found the address of Harrelson Long and Son, Esq. in Colorado Springs. Wondering if she'd be lucky enough to get out in time to make the venue by four thirty and meet Dawn, she refreshed her lip gloss, fluffed the head full of hair that was beginning to look like an overly loved pet.

Genevieve's visit had delayed her already tight schedule. Her visit with Jesse morphed into a phone call. Jesse was more upbeat now that Pedro passed the first wave of interrogations and was being represented by an attorney who Riley recommended. It looked as if he might be released and home as early as tonight, although he was still a person of interest in the eyes of the law.

Candace and Jesse both agreed it was unlikely Pedro would harm Dan, but in his drunken stupor, he couldn't remember where he had been hours before the attack. His alibi thankfully ending up being a one-horse town drunk tank located between the ranch and El Paso.

What a day and what awful timing to see Tripp for the first time in nine years, but she had no choice. For the past two hours on the drive from Gallegos to Colorado Springs, countless butterflies had taken up residence in her stomach. By the time the secretary announced her arrival and after giving her the once over with cautious eyes, Candace felt she might throw up. Bolting for the outside door seemed like a good idea.

Tripp was just getting out of his chair to walk around his desk when Candace was shown into the room. He slipped on a light gray suit jacket that had be draped across the high-backed leather chair in one slick, effortless motion as he crossed the room. Older but still fit, his arms bulged against the coat sleeves. He straightened his charcoal and black striped tie, which was no doubt was made of silk.

Her heart began to pound, and her breaths shortened.

Growing up without her father, Uncle Dan was her one and only male role model through high school. Men were an enigma from the start, and Tripp Long had been her first serious flirtation and a big secret. Uncle knew she had had contemplated beginning her culinary training early but never guessed what actually prompted her departure from college.

The antithesis of Anton, a shorter, stockier version of his foreign counterpart, Tripp spent most of his time buried in books containing case law and legalese. Anton was all about volumes of recipes and practicing the art of coaxing flavors from sinewy animal flesh and creating succulent textures from a mere pinch of a seasoning.

Unlike the carefree devil-may-care attitude Anton oozed into her daily life, Tripp was a level-headed conservative, and a reserved and thoughtful man. Anton, years younger than Candace, was comfortable with the idea of clawing and scratching his way to the top whereas Tripp was already there, raised in affluence with the trappings attained by old family money.

Tripp extended his hand to her. She accepted his hand deftly, as if greeting one of her clients, but once their palms connected, the familiar electricity sparked between them. They both held the grip firmly. Their eyes locked in a warm welcoming gaze and they shared a smile, one that assured the other the time between them had nearly stood still.

Tripp broke the handshake and weighty silence by wrapping his arms around her in a strong but brief hug. Dropping one arm, he steered her comfortably toward a trio of burgundy leather chairs grouped around a coffee table. For a moment, it was as if they were dancing, though there was no music. Her knees wobbled.

"Is this okay?" He motioned to the chair next to the roaring fireplace. Colorado temperatures and the windy late afternoon had turned brisk.

Her knees still wobbled and a shiver passed down her spine. "Fine, thanks."

"I am so sorry about Dan and what you must be going through," he started. "But it's really good to see you."

"It's okay. He's going to be fine. I just know it!" She couldn't admit how incredible it was to lay eyes on Tripp after all these years. How can people drift apart so easily and never cross paths even when living in neighboring cities?

"Dad said he spoke with you about the will. I have a copy of it in our files." As Tripp spoke, he was studying her face. "I also have a copy of his DNR for you."

She wondered what he was thinking as she felt his eyes on her. "Thanks, but as I said, I'm sure we won't need it."

He politely changed the subject. "What, if anything, are the police saying?"

"It's been a crazy couple of days. At first, they insisted Uncle must have fallen or collapsed. Now, they've finally decided it wasn't an accident but are trying to charge Jesse's son with attempted murder." She waited for his reaction.

"Do they have evidence to support that?" he asked the question with the embodied discretion of an attorney.

Candace went on to tell him everything. She relived the night she found Dan and detailed his injury. She recalled Merlin's death and what the vet told her about the poisoning, Sam's ongoing police investigation, and lastly, rubbing salt into the wound, Pedro's arrest and Genevieve's appearance.

"Tripp listened in silence, never taking his gaze from her face. Well, it sounds to me as if the sheriff could be onto something. I know how close you are to Jesse, but how well do you know her son?"

"Pretty well, I mean he's spent time at the ranch, but his dad practically raised him since Jesse was always with us. You know, Tripp, it makes me feel responsible in a way. Jesse gave more of herself to me and Uncle than to her own family."

"I know. But remember, CJ, everyone makes those types of choices and for their own reasons. Commitment comes with a cost." He looked at her evenly.

Was he talking about their choices in college? Their unspoken, under-discussed decision of letting go after all they'd felt for each other?

Was it the overall situation with Uncle or seeing Tripp again that suddenly made her so sad? Eyes filling with tears she diverted attention to her cell phone clock, the large digital numbers on the screen virtually screamed that a speedy departure was imminent. How could she leave after such a short visit?

She remembered something Jesse had told her. "Tripp, the sheriff is asking around about my relationship with Uncle and also about my business partner Anton."

"Do you know what type of questions he's asking?"

She nodded. "Yes, about the money Uncle allowed me to pull from my trust for the business."

"That's within his scope, but I'd be careful about answering too many questions without counsel. Sounds like he's on a fishing expedition, but you can't be too careful. Dad and I can't represent you, conflict of interest and all, but I will get you hooked up with one of my buddies."

Candace added, "He also asked about my agreement with Anton and his percentage of the catering business."

"That's a subject I can field. Didn't my dad draw up those papers?"

Between Tripp's close presence and the fire, she was parched. "Yes, about five years ago."

"I thought so. So, he's sniffing around Anton, huh?" The tiny muscle on the inside of his cheek flexed.

"Yes, but that's just ridiculous."

"Still, I'd like to know what connection he thinks there might be to him with regard to your uncle. Is this sheriff in Gallegos?"

She nodded.

"Look, if anyone asks you about the contracts between the two of you, refer them to me." Tripp stared at her intently. "Would you like some coffee?"

She reminded him about her upcoming event and the reason she needed to cut short their time together. Leaving was a less than attractive option. Both sat attentively leaning into the other, eyes penetrating, deep in thought. They were emotionally, intellectually and physically focused on each other and the emotions at hand. Ending the meeting was like peeling skin from the flesh of a grape.

"I want you to call me with any news–any time at all." He reached for a business card out of the table top holder and scribbled something quickly on the back. "Here's my card. My personal cell is on the back."

They were face-to-face as they stood.

"Thanks, Tripp. It really was good seeing you again." She had to give him that. "I appreciate all your help, and tell your dad I said 'hi.'"

He kissed her cheek with his palms clutching her upper arms. "I will. He's going to see Dan tomorrow."

"You should, too." Her words swallowed themselves and filled her throat. She wondered how he had been all these years, and if he had someone special in his life.

Candace was grateful for the chilled wind that met her warm cheeks when she scurried out of the building. It made the flush that bloomed there look almost natural. For now, she was off to Denver to work. She left Tripp inside on the phone to Gallegos.

CHAPTER 19

Candace knew the first order of business at the venue for Anton was to properly arrange the mansion's dining room. Tonight was typical. Tables, chairs and linens were dropped off by the rental company, without specific instruction. They were merely piled in the vestibule along with the other deliveries. Flower arrangements were in the hallway stacked in boxes.

She walked onto the scene and it became like a ballroom waltz. Candace shifted into set-up mode, an action she was confident handling. "Ro, can you make sure the floral arrangements and loose flowers for the buffet are put under refrigeration please? And let's get eight chairs at each one of those tables. The color scheme is silver on purple, guys."

She looked around, thinking. Four on the floor already and three working on setting up the kitchen and they still might not be ready on time. "Zach, you and Ro are on tablecloths and napkins and buffet set-up. Kayla, you and the new guy take charge of flatware, then hook up for the water glasses. I'll make sure your things come off the truck first."

"Anton?" Kayla called from across the room seeing him walk in. "Are we providing water goblets for this one?"

Anton shot Candace a brilliant smile and wink as he grabbed a stack of plates. "No, but Dawn said she ordered all the glasses for the tables along with the one's for the bar."

"Okay, I'll find them," Kayla responded. She was one of their favorite servers. Sharp and well trained, she looked calm and professional in her crisp white shirt and short black skirt. Her hair was pulled into a ponytail and her comfortable black nursing shoes allowed her to work quickly and stealthily, filling in where others left off.

"Anton, where do you want the chocolate fountain?" asked Zach, always organized. He was another favorite staffer who was in fact preparing to transition into banquet manager. Like Anton, he was tall and imposing, but the comparison ended abruptly at his short-cropped strawberry blonde hair, fair skin and freckles, more resembling Prince Harry, the third in line to the British throne. His attire was typical: a pair of sharply creased tuxedo pants, a crisp black dress shirt with the embroidered To Dine For Catering logo, a black tie and a smooth ankle-length black apron tied at the waist signified his level of importance among the group.

Anton acknowledged him with a directive nod toward the library door. That's all the information Zach would need to set up a lavish presentation. Candace loved watching Anton at work and the moments like this that proved she made a good choice in their partnership.

"Hey, boss," Zach addressed Anton again. "How 'bout the ice? Who got it, them or us?"

"We did. It's in one of the big storage coolers," Anton answered as he disappeared behind the swinging kitchen door. Candace was confident the dining room would be transformed in short order and reveal a stunning example of their hard work and attention to detail. Several hundred square feet adorned by oil paintings and lit up by chandeliers would be embellished by hundreds of candles and lavish decorations. Serving sounds and conversation would be cloaked with lilting chords of piped in music through-out. A violin trio scheduled to play during dinner hour was arriving shortly. They had a really great team.

Candace released her grip on center stage long enough to switch her focus to the crates of dishes, pots, pans and boxes of food stuffs. Anyone not in jeans or black logoed t-shirts were excluded from this area until "show" time. Poles apart, the kitchen staff were the antithesis of service staff. Servers dressed to impress were banished while food prep was underway. Hot boxes and coolers opened, flames ignited, stations were set up with raw food and organized chaos reigned. No wonder the military labeled anything to do with food service "mess."

Once everyone was in motion, she donned her black executive chef's coat which she wore over her bright red chef pants. She tied a clean black apron tightly around her slender mid-section after procuring the case containing her coveted knives. Sharpened perfectly, they were her fine-tuned instruments of imple-mentation.

Sorting, finishing, plating and staging were underway. Sauce ingredients stood at the ready. Hot dishes arrived in portable heated boxes which traveled with them to events and kept the temperature of food at a constant and safe 160 degrees.

"We're plating the salads so clear some space everyone," Cameron commanded. Cam's girl, Bri, fell in comfortably behind him to coordinate. As capable as she was pretty, she quietly led the charge for the appetizers.

"The shrimp shooters will go out first," Candace reminder her. "Do we have the garlic aioli?"

"Yep, made it before we left," Cameron chimed in.

The entire production was tantamount to a captain leading troops into battle, and Anton and Candace both had respective and complementary skills for it.

Amidst the confusion, no one noticed Dawn appear. She

descended from the service staircase and looked as put together as a guest rather than the organizer.

She was seductively poured into a dark purple cocktail dress with a bodice slit down the front to the waist. Borrowed from Candace she jazzed it up with a stunning faux diamond necklace and a glittery rhinestone buckle at the waist. Her hair was the crowning touch, sleek and shiny. Once again, Dawn had most surely out dressed any woman on the invitation list. Not a word passed between them about the previous night.

Bri took time from cutting lettuce to sneak next to Candace. "How are you? How is your uncle?" Her voice showed obvious concern. She was a very pretty, very tiny version of Candace but with short, shiny brown hair streaked with cobalt blue. Brianna was all about fashion and detail and loved to fuss with food. She could curl a carrot or charm a tomato into a rose with the best of any professional *garde manger,* who produced vegetable carvings and ice figurines.

"I'm okay, really." Candace insisted and smiled sweetly. "There's still no change. I wish he could see us marching on and taking care of business."

She smiled at Anton who had joined the conversation and nearly bent himself in half to gently kiss the inside of her palm. A gesture of such respect and adoration she had to choke back a sob.

Bri stood by to sneak another hug, and Anton peered squinting at the rest of the staff as if to say "get back to work!" Candace embraced Bri reassuringly and winked at the room. They would all get their shot at her later.

Anton crossed the kitchen announcing over his shoulder as if he were Captain Kirk turning over the bridge of the Enterprise to Spock. "I'm going to check the dining room. Cam, it's all yours!"

Candace stopped to inspect Cam's work and adjusted the parmesan crisp sitting on the side of the plate but seemed otherwise satisfied.

"If you didn't tweak something, it wouldn't be you." His cheeks reddened, and his eyes filled when she looked into them.

"Now, no waterworks in the salad. It'll ruin the dressing." She grinned and winked at him.

Cam rarely let the pressure get to him, and if it did, he kept a bag of marijuana buds handy to compensate. As long as he didn't light up during an event, Anton and Candace were cool with it. Cam was devoted to the work and to Bri. Cooking since he was a young child, he only truly embraced his love for it once he and his mom became Candace's neighbors. Still in high school, he hung out at the kitchen whenever possible to watch, listen, and absorb whatever morsels of the catering business he could. Candace often bragged to her uncle that Cam was "going places." She just knew it.

Candace followed Anton out the door that swung in his wake.

If she hadn't done this hundreds, possibly thousands of times, she might only see what others did when they walked into the room. A glittering spectacle of silver and crystal, satin tablecloths, shiny dishes and flickering candlelight was breathtaking. Chairs were covered in the same heavy, silver brocade fabric that matched the tablecloths, and large purple satin bows were tied on the back of each one in a color identical to the napkins. Kayla had polished each of the one-hundred-fifty individual place settings to a sparkle. Baby lilac-tinted Chrysanthemum buds adorned each napkin tied with an ivory ribbon. Ample arrangements of purple Anthuriums and Iris with tiny daisies, pulled from refrigerator storage, flocked the center of the tables.

Candace viewed every party scene from a different angle, one that made her the renowned caterer she was, and that was the angle she reinforced in Anton, Zach and Cam with every function. Were all the tablecloths dropped at an exact and even space from the floor? Did all place settings have the proper flatware, seafood and salad forks, butter and steak knives, soup and dessert-coffee spoons, and were they all positioned correctly? Was each chair in front of each setting and just far enough away from the table to allow the cloth to hang free? Were the water glasses filled with ice? Enough butter pats in the dishes? Were there any scraps of paper, clips, hangers or rubber bands from rentals lying on the floor? Was anything the client ordered missing? Candace surveyed the plates, centerpieces in place, napkins folded, everything neat, clean and tidy, including the servers.

"We need to get the table markers in place," Anton called out, to no one in particular, and everyone in general.

"Doing that now," Zach called back.

"You've all done a great job! I didn't doubt you for a minute." Candace called out attracting attention once again. She thought it best to get all sentiment out of the way before guests started to arrive. As expected, they huddled around her like a football team surrounding their coach. Some gave out handshakes and well wishes, and others swarmed her with hugs and gushing sentiments.

"We've got about ten minutes to passing, and we'll serve in thirty," Anton called out. Candace had to admit he sounded just like her. His command worked to break up all the well-wishers.

Zach announced with authority, probably more for his own benefit since he was one of the few smokers left in the group, "Anyone who needs to change or wants a smoke, do it now."

"Let's get this show on the road, guys!" Candace chimed in looking at the time and snuck back in the kitchen to grab a bite of her sandwich.

Dawn had vanished up the stairs with own like a sequestered bride to return once the festivities were underway. As guests poured into the foyer and lined up at the bar, devoured trays of appetizers were refilled, and Dawn made her grand entrance down the formal staircase when the congressman arrived. Peacock perfect, the pair proceeded to strut arm in arm around the room preening their intricately patterned physiques, keeping precise posture.

The staff and owners of To Dine For Catering were in their element. Satisfying the desires of every guest, executing course after course of exquisitely presented menu items, they spiriting away any tell-tale signs in the aftermath. Women of substance danced with the potential candidate while their male counterparts armed with checkbooks gathered under the outdoor cabana trellis to light up everything from cigarettes to cigars and small glass pipes packed full with recently legalized marijuana.

Dawn was huddled among those whose pockets were as full of money as the evening air was trailed with smoke. Liquor served in the form of shots and fancier concoctions flowed along with beer and champagne; all guzzled into the wee hours.

A skeleton staff stayed until after one o'clock, but the remainder bugged out with the equipment and dirty dishes in tow. After every event, every serving piece, every scrap of food was to be removed from the location and brought back to the offices. Breakdown was as intricate as set up had been.

Candace could do all of this orchestration and production with such ease, but what would she do without Uncle? Working and keeping busy filled the time, but she felt like a loose end. The feeling of loneliness was palpable. Tripp had possessed a piece of her heart for a time, Anton would always have a special place but Uncle–he was at the center. He helped Candace feel, dream and reach for the stars. He was her everything.

On her way back to the kitchen, she vowed not to give up.

CHAPTER 20

Post-event at To Dine For Catering offices was a special time. The cacophony of clanging dishes, tinkling glasses in their carriers and the voices of the breakdown staff kicking the second shift into high gear was music to her ears. The harmony meant another successful job well done and money in the bank.

Candace knew that right this minute a small group of night owls familiar with back alleys, loading docks and loud music were gathering for a quick smoke before spending the better part of the early morning hours washing, cleaning, organizing, and inventorying everything she owned. These people were a bread unto themselves. Grateful for the work and the chance to grab a sip of wine from discarded bottles and to scarf down bites of leftover cake and hors d'oeuvres, these workers were an important cog in the catering wheel.

Anton popped around the corner into her office. "Hey you."

"Hey yourself. Wanna join me?" Candace motioned to the couch on which Anton proceeded to collapse, kicking off his work shoes and elevating his feet on the coffee table.

Candace's stocking-covered feet were already propped on her

desk edge. "I just hung up with the hospital. Uncle has been resting quietly no thanks to his several visitors."

"Visitors?"

"Well, attempted visitors. They're still not allowing anyone except immediate family, you, Dawn, and the sheriff of course, but that woman Genevieve came by again. Plus another woman who didn't leave her name. Oddly enough, my aunt Marjorie, was also there. Dawn never mentioned her mom was coming to town. Anyway, she wasn't too happy about the rules and even tried to bribe the nurse. She left in a huff when that didn't work and said she'd be back in a few days. I wonder why she didn't just call me."

"Yeah, that is strange."

Commotion from the kitchen drowned out what he said next, and Candace inquired about it.

"I said, what a night! he answered, raising his voice. "I think Dawn hit on every eligible bachelor in the place."

"No doubt sharpening her pencil and extracting everything she could from them. The congressman's lucky to have her." Candace rocked back in her chair. She loosened her hair to let in fall to her shoulders.

"Well, he can have her." Anton seemed to hesitate. "I know you have a history with her, but I almost hate to have her associated with us."

"She's a go-getter alright but harmless."

"That's my point. She goes out of her way to get them and to be gotten like a high-class hooker." He cocked his head toward her and raised an eyebrow.

Candace scoffed. "I'm surprised at you. That's such an old-fashioned way of thinking."

Anton made his way around the back of the chair and began rubbing her shoulders. "I just don't like her. She uses your reputation to further hers."

She yawned and stretched her neck from side to side. "That feels great. I'll keep her at a safe distance, I promise."

Shifting the conversation toward the focal points of the night, she recounted the many compliments the elite showered upon her, and she singled out each contact she made. This was their time to compare notes. Anton chattered on about the dishes served, their presentation, the good and bad of the orchestration of the evening from his point of view.

Anton swiveled around and leaned against the edge of her desk taking one foot and kneading her toes like bread dough. "You know, we need to make sure we get final approval and a sign off from the host in advance from now on. The congressman was really concerned about the menu and our services. He said he hadn't been given a copy of the menu for final approval."

"That's an odd thing to say. Dawn had a date with him this past weekend to go over everything, but he stood her up and went out of town. How can he blame us?"

Anton muttered, "That's not what he said. He told me he tried to see her before he left, but she had something come up. He didn't hear from her until a phone call a few days later right before your walk through."

"Hmmm. When Dawn showed up at the hospital, she told me that their plans changed, so she went to the movies." This wasn't sitting right with Candace.

"You see what I mean? You can't believe a thing she says. Let's send a staffer next time or fax it to the client, okay?"

"Fine with me," she said but began to play that night over in her mind. Why would Dawn lie about her date? What had she really been doing?

"Are you heading back in the morning or coming in?" Anton asked when the conversation waned.

"I'll go straight down in the morning and see the sheriff and Jesse if I can, then go to the hospital. I'll be back tomorrow night." She sighed thinking about the drive again.

"Do you want me to join you? I'd like to see Dan tomorrow."

"You could. His attorney is coming to visit as well as his son Tripp."

Anton had heard her mention the name before. "Oh, he's been in touch?"

"Yes, as a matter of fact, I saw him earlier today." Candace was certain that statement would go over like a ton of bricks.

"I see." Anton stood up placing her foot back on the desk. He stretched, arms over his head and twisted his waist. He grasped one elbow then the other until his back cracked in release. His jacket lifted above his belt to reveal his washboard stomach covered in fine hair. "I guess I'll go down tomorrow night or Sunday after the brunch. I think I'll skip meeting the old boyfriend."

Despite it being a relief, she asked coyly, "Jealous?" Then bit her lip.

The two never talked much about their feelings. Anton flirted a lot with her in culinary school and all the girls really. Her relationship with him was more cerebral, but there was an undeniable attraction. It crept in, revealing itself when she least expected it, but neither of them were prepared to handle it.

In three years, she never questioned their feelings for each other and credited the electricity between them to the adrenaline rush of event orchestration. When complete exhaustion erased any pretenses, their physical contact, although platonic, was natural and relaxing. Back, neck and foot massages, legs and arms entangled, or heads resting in laps became habit.

"Jealousy is for those with no bones in their backs," he stated firmly and started for the door.

She thought for a moment and smiled. "No backbone?"

"Right. I have a backbone, no jealousy. I'm going to check on the guys, and I'll be in my office until they're done."

The trill of the desk phone ringing broke the tension. Candace took the call as Anton paused in the doorway.

She cried out after barely saying goodbye to the cheerful nurse on the other end of the line. "Anton! He's awake. Uncle's awake!"

Clinging to the door frame by the hinges, Anton spoke quickly, "What? How? When?"

Candace laughed. Whoever would have thought Anton could translate his Russian thoughts into English so quickly?

"The nurse said he simply woke up." Her face gleamed, tears welling in her eyes. She rushed across the room and flung herself into his outstretched arms. "They're checking his vitals now but he's off the respirator and talking. He's actually talking, Anton!"

"That is *klassno!*" Anton hugged her tightly. "Let's go!"

It didn't matter the time, how far it was or how tired they were. Candace grabbed her purse and golden-threaded paisley shawl to wrap around the crimson dress she wore after the function to schmooze with the clients. She scooted down the marble hall into the foyer, skidding haltingly on the balls of her feet to avoid sliding off her high heels.

"This is probably the best night of my whole life. I can't even breathe." Hand to her chest, she practiced a calming yoga technique to quell the beginnings of hyperventilation. "We can finally find out what happened!"

"We should bring something to celebrate with, yes?" Anton asked while snatching a bottle of his favorite Russian vodka.

"Umm, I don't know, they may not even let him drink it. Doesn't matter, let's go. No one's with him, and I'd hate him to think he was left all alone."

"I think he knows better." Anton chuckled at her delight, shut the lights down, set the alarm and locked the front door. "We'll have no unwelcome visitors tonight."

She didn't understand what he meant. "What?"

"Oh, nothing, we just need to be more careful to lock up at night. We never know who could come in uninvited," he cautioned but said no more.

"Okay, whatever you say." She dismissed it with a wave. Her

only concern was to get to her uncle's side. "The crew will be here anyway."

"Oh, we need to call Jesse, and then Dawn, of course, and the papers will want a statement," she announced as her feet hit the bottom step. "Ugh, I hate all this. Maybe I should ask Dawn to handle it."

"She rubs reporters the wrong way, and then they dig around trying to check her story. They don't trust her. She uses them and misleads them all the time. Do you remember the story she made up last month? She should go to work for a tabloid." He helped her into the low seat of his Porsche 911.

"I suppose."

Seated behind the wheel, Anton continued as Candace penned a list, "The reporters, they like you, not just you, but your uncle as well."

She was barely listening to Anton. "I need to contact his partners, the ranch hands, his friends. Oh–Tripp and his dad, too." She smiled, rolling her eyes and resting her head on the seat back. She felt relaxed for the first time in a week. "We've got a couple of hours, yet. So I won't worry about it now. Everyone is asleep anyway. Thanks for being here."

She reached out and held his hand.

He took it and squeezed, then transferred his grasp to the shift. They pulled away from the inner-city streets heading south on the highway which would take them out of Colorado in less than two hours the way Anton was driving. He turned on some classic rock and played it softly.

CHAPTER 21

Dan's eyelids lifted slowly, exposing the world around him. Dimly lit and unrecognizable, the room was cavernous. The walls were bare, painted an antiseptic white. The ceiling was riddled with metal supports. Wires and equipment hung from every angle. Large machines beeped and hissed in an eerie rhythm, like percussion instruments in a slow jazz band. His head was heavy, too heavy to turn and his arms wouldn't move on command. He was cold. The plastic obstruction that held his mouth open made his lips dry and didn't allow him to speak.

He bent his knees and rolled his thighs without difficulty. He wiggled his toes. His body was functioning unrestricted with the exception of thick footless stockings that covered his lower legs and constricted every few minutes, keeping pace with the automatic blood pressure cuff on his arm.

He was alive and in one piece. What the hell happened? He could tell he was in a hospital. Probably an intensive care unit, no frills. He had the benefit of cognitive reasoning. That was a good sign.

The room was sterile, no furniture save one chair and no television. His nose itched. Determined to move an arm, he concentrated on making it happen. He reached to touch his face and throbbing head. Nothing else seemed to hurt but that. Had he been in an accident? What day of the week was it? What month or year for that matter?

He looked at the IV in his right arm and the bags of liquid tethered to it from above. Fluids, that was good, but he could use a little morphine right about then. He remembered talking with Dawn over a glass of wine. The situation with her mother was a mess. She was still carrying around so much hate.

What on earth could have brought him there?

The mere motion trying to touch his face made him lose strength, and his arm fell mid-movement back to the bed, sending off warning bells and chimes. A flurry of people in hospital scrubs and nurse's uniforms filled the room, overhead lights glowed ablaze like stadium lights as though they were ready to highlight the first pitch. Concerned faces turned to smiles and quiet whispers became commanding, authoritative voices. "Mr. Kane...Dan? Can you move your toes? The other foot. Good!"

"Your hands? Raise your arm? Good!"

He had done all that already. *You guys missed it*, he thought. *In case you were wondering, my head hurts like hell.*

There was a nurse or doctor at each extremity. Others were hurrying with charts and rolling carts stacked with vials and needles. One man started taking blood from an IV port. Another checked his pulse on his feet and ankles.

"Mr. Kane, I'm Dr.Garcia. *Buenas noches*, sir."

A doctor. What a relief.

"You're in Gallegos General Hospital. You were brought here after being hurt in your home four and a half days ago. You've been in a coma. Do you understand?"

Dan nodded slightly. If they would just get the thing out of his throat then maybe he could talk to them and ask questions about what was going on.

"Can you look to the left, sir?"

He looked, but couldn't see anything. The little light was too bright.

"Now, follow the light please, sir. Up...down...now to the right...to the left. Good, good."

Enough with the parlor tricks. Now what? Dan was getting annoyed.

"Alright, you're looking good. Now we're going to take that respirator out of your mouth. Can you help me out here, Mr. Kane?"

Dan offered a thumbs up.

A group of scrubbed hands hovered around his head. Dr. Garcia's voice boomed, "Okay, Mr. Kane. On the count of three, I want you to give me a big cough. Ready? 1, 2, 3!"

Dan coughed and heaved. The white tube came out of him with a tug. It seemed the whole room exhaled a collective sigh of relief as he took in his first breath on his own.

The doc calling the shots was obviously quite familiar with this procedure. "Don't try to talk just yet, Mr. Kane. It's going to be uncomfortable at first. The nurse will be giving you some ice chips in a minute."

"How are we doing, sir?" A nurse patted Dan on the shoulder.

He was just told not to talk, now they were asking him how he was? He'd been better, that's for sure. He wondered what accident they were referring to. He would remember something that made his head feel like this.

An angel of a girl with doe eyes, a little younger than Candace, placed a plastic spoon against his lips. Ice chips. Dan nodded.

The cold hard particles melted quickly into cool soothing water. He cringed upon swallowing but took more.

"Candace?" He finally got a word out. His voice was raspy and indiscernible.

"Sir?"

Great, she didn't catch it the first time.

"Candace?" he whispered and then the memories came

rushing back.

He remembered calling Candace, and he'd had such an argument with Dawn. She had stormed out of the house, dogs running after her, but Candace was at work in the mountains. Then everything went black, and there he was.

Another woman stepped close to his side dressed in scrubs. Her dark red hair was pulled up under a paper cap with a green face mask hooked over her ears. "Mr. Kane? I'm Dr. Menendez. Glad to have you back! I believe you're asking about your niece. She's been here on and off since your accident, but I understand she had to return to Denver today. Someone has already placed a call to let her know you are awake."

Her eyes seemed to smile at him from above the mask, and he imagined they were the color of moss.

Dan nodded and attempted a smile. He winced ever so slightly.

"Are you experiencing pain, Mr. Kane?"

He nodded again. "My head," he croaked.

"Ah, yes. Your head suffered quite a trauma. Let me get you set up on something for that. Can we get morphine on his IV?" she looked at a nurse nearby. She returned her attention to him. "Are you feeling any other pain right now?"

My back, my ass. I must have fallen on my ass. "Not really." He struggled to speak. "Nothing your morphine won't cure. Thank you, doctor. Do you know who brought me here?"

"An ambulance, and I'm told your niece came in right after that."

One at a time, the scrub-dressed coalition emptied from the room like ants retreating from a disturbed pile. Within minutes Dan was alone again, the lights were switched off as he felt the floating sensation of medication coursing through his veins. Through the window, the sky turned shades of navy and dark purple as the sun gave birth to a new day. In a few hours, it would peek above the horizon.

It would be damned good to see sun again.

CHAPTER 22

A s they sped toward the hospital, Anton cleared his throat and
said, ""CJ, speaking of Dawn, I need to discuss something
with you I've been trying to steer clear of since before the event."

She grinned gazing at him. "What did she do now? Sneak into
the kitchen and make the staff crazy?"

"No, nothing like that. I don't really know where to begin or
how to explain." He began again.

She patted his hand. "Anton, I know you can't stand her, but
she *did* land us the congressman's event. That was a nice piece of
change, even with the deal we gave them. Look, whatever it is, I'll
call her now, tell her about Uncle, and she can meet us at the
hospital. Then you two can 'make nice.'"

"No!" He smacked his hand on the leather steering wheel
cover.

Candace pulled away from him sharply. She'd never seen him
behave like this except the rare occasions when something
curdled or burned in the kitchen.

"Anton, what's wrong?"

He frowned. "I'm sorry, I cannot lay eyes on her tonight!"

"Okay, what happened? It must have really been something." She could feel her face flush.

Anton paused as if building up confidence.

She waited patiently, feeling a lump form in her throat. "Anton, it can't be that bad."

"Oh yes it can," he responded, his face stoic. "Candace, the other night when you stayed down in Gallegos, the night Dawn was at our office?"

"Yes. Are you still mad that she ordered take out and left it all over the dining room? I told her to *never* do that again!"

"No, I am not mad. I think she's a fool, but I am not angry about that." He took in a deep breath. "CJ, I was there. I mean, I wasn't there when she ordered the food but before that. I drove by, saw the lights and her car in the driveway."

She looked puzzled. "And you let her in?"

"No, *no*, she was already in your office. She said the front door was unlocked, and she wanted to pick up your dress. Anyway, when I found her, she was in your closet, and before I knew it, she was...she was all over me."

"All over you?" His words echoed in her head.

"Yes, she seduced me. She threw herself at me, and we well, we had sex." He paused and looked at her briefly then back to the windshield.

"In our *offices?*" She recalled the minor disarray in her office. "Wait, *my* office?" Her voice came out shriller than she expected.

"Mm-hmm." He nodded, lips pulled taut and stared at the empty road ahead.

Candace sat quietly, taking it all in. She was bothered by it, but she didn't even know if she had the right to be. Was she mad at him? At Dawn? Her own self? She just wasn't sure what to do with it all.

"CJ, I'm sorry. I am so sorry." He huffed. "It was completely unexpected, and I didn't do anything to, to..."

"Lead her on? No, I wouldn't imagine you did. But Anton, what *did* you do?"

"God, Candace, she's the last woman on earth I want to be with. You know that, but it was late, I was tired, and she was dressed to kill, and it had been a while. I tried to fight it, but I guess I'm only Russian."

Quiet ruled the car again except for the strains of "music for lover's" melodies coming from the speakers.

Anton finally blurted out. "Candace, say something!"

"You mean human," she said evenly as she'd done many times before.

"What?"

"You meant human, not Russian. You're only human." She paused again, trying to play it cool. "Oh, Anton, I don't know what to say. I'm not your girlfriend, and I'm certainly not your mother, but I am your partner, and I would have thought you would show more discretion."

"Dis-cre-shon?' He sounded the word out phonetically while he translated. "You mean made a better choice?"

She snapped at him crossing her arms locking them in front of her. "That too!"

Minutes ticked by as they watched road signs fly past aglow in the headlights and fireflies hit the windshield.

Anton reached over and pulled the bottle out from between the gear shift and his thigh. He unscrewed the cap with his teeth, and threw his head back, taking a big swig.

"Want some?" he asked tilting the bottle in her direction.

She wasn't pleased with his confession or his drinking while driving. Her emotions in the last hour had reached some real highs and lows. She took the bottle, filled her mouth, letting the vodka burn her tongue and slide down her throat. She shuddered.

CJ, I will never touch her again. I can't even believe I did it the first time. I'm really sorry for the choice, the discretion...all of it."

She drew in another swig, handed the bottle back and faced

the window, putting an end to the conversation. A tear traveled down her cheek. She felt betrayed, but she didn't know by whom.

The remainder of the trip went by in silence, and thankfully Anton didn't drink any more vodka. She was ready to put this all behind her. She needed to keep her head in the game, make sure they got to the hospital safely and find out what really happened to Dan.

CHAPTER 23

Tiptoeing into the room, Candace immediately noticed the sound of the machines had ceased. It was quiet and barely lit. Uncertain as to his condition, she made her way to her uncle's bedside and hesitated for a moment. He must have sensed her as his eyes flew open.

"Come here young lady, I won't bite." His voice sounded shaky and raspy, but he broke into a smile. He had returned to her.

Tears welled, and her whole body felt weak with relief. "Oh my God! I didn't know if you would ever wake up, Uncle." She kissed him on his forehead twice, his cheek several times, and then all over the back of his hand like a bumble bee resting ever so briefly then flitting off to another sweet spot.

"Now that's just the sort of welcome back an old man needs!" he whispered, lacing it with as much frivolity as one could muster after what he'd been through.

Anton cheerfully stepped up to the bed and grabbed Dan's other hand firmly. "You're a sight for sore eyes, old man. What were you thinking, scaring us all like that?"

Candace agreed. "I was scared to death, Uncle."

"Now, now. There was no need to be afraid. You can't get rid of me that easy." He tried to reassure them, but Candace could see the confusion and concern in his eyes. "What happened anyway?"

Candace frowned. "You don't remember?"

"I assumed an accident of some sort put me in here. But why don't I remember it?"

"You were attacked," she blurted then corrected herself. "Or fell. You called me to come down to the ranch, and when I got there, you were on the floor bleeding. That was over four days ago. You've been in a coma ever since."

"We don't know if you were attacked or if it was an accident. We were hoping you could tell us. Did you surprise a burglar or something?" The question was posed by Anton gently but urgently.

Uncle Dan seemed to think about it for a minute. "I don't recall any attack or anything else that would put me here."

Dr. Melendez entered the room. "That's quite a normal reaction from patients with blunt force trauma to the head. We find the memory of an event connected to this type of injury is sketchy at best. It may fully return over time, but it might not."

Candace was disappointed. "So, you don't remember anything?"

"The last thing I remember was being home Saturday evening. I was going through some papers I had found in the attic. There were boxes of some pictures and letters from years ago."

"We found them." Candace squeezed his hand. She could not bring herself to let go.

"Then–" He stared off into space. "Then Dawn came over, and we had some wine."

Candace nearly shouted. "Dawn? Dawn came to the ranch by herself?"

Hat in hand, Sheriff Sam stepped into the room and made his way to the bedside. "Excuse me, Mr. Kane. I must request you withhold any further information on the night in question until we interview you. I need to create a timeline of events and get a first-hand account."

Dan shook the sheriff's hand and shrugged. "Certainly Sam, but that's all I remember. It's good to see you, son."

The doctor warned, "There will be no interviews or questioning for at least another twenty-four hours. And, I need you to get some rest, Mr. Kane."

"But doctor, I have an open investigation. Waiting will only impede it," the sheriff objected.

"And," the doctor added. "For the next day or two, there'll be only one visitor at a time for Mr. Kane. Immediate family only. He's been through quite an ordeal."

"But, doc...," Sam began.

"Sheriff, that's final. My concern is for my patient, not your investigation." She reached for Dan's wrist and felt for his vital signs. "In fact, everyone in this room who's not immediate family really needs to step out *now*." A firm emphasis was placed on the end of her edict.

Anton directed. "You heard the doctor. Let's go."

They filed out like soldiers under command as Candace plopped down on the springy stool. She whispered to Uncle, "Why did Dawn come to the ranch when I was in Denver? She was supposed to be meeting with the congressman about the fundraiser."

"I called her that afternoon. You know, she really is such a sad young lady," he paused and gazed thoughtfully. "I told her I was cleaning out the attic, and if she wanted anything, she could come down. I found a bunch of boxes with items from when you kids were there during the summer."

"I know, when I got there it looked like someone had been rummaging through everything for a specific purpose. There were files of pictures and letters all over the floor and chairs."

Uncle Dan's eyes narrowed. "You don't say. I don't think Dawn would be very happy about anyone reading or keeping her letters."

"Her letters? Well, I went through them and organized the mess but couldn't tell if anything was missing."

"Yes, that's one reason I called Dawn. I'm not sure how they got there or even if she's read them. I do know she was pretty upset with me when she saw them, but I guess I was lucky she was there after all. Did she call the paramedics?"

Candace considered the details before responding and shared an edited version. Dawn hadn't gotten him to a hospital. In fact, she never admitted to being there. Candace told him about the door being ajar but didn't think her uncle was strong enough to accept Merlin's death. Not yet.

Candace asked him, "Why was Dawn upset with you?"

"I wouldn't give her the letters. I wanted to speak with your aunt Marjorie first. Some of the content was pretty personal and should be left in the past. I hadn't read all of them, but some of what I did read was even news to me."

"So... she came down, and then what?" Candace was prodding but wanted to tread lightly.

"We had some wine."

"That explains the two wine glasses."

Uncle Dan shook his head. "But that's where I draw a blank. We were arguing, and she left in a huff, Lance and Merlin ran after her, but I don't remember what happened to me. What happened?"

Candace methodically revealed the rest of the story as much as she felt safe to recall. Her uncle's eyes went from shock to surprise, then acceptance and sadness. He admitted he could barely stomach the distress the whole event must have caused Candace.

He gripped her hand. "Honey, if all this happened because I called Dawn over some old letters, I'll never forgive myself!"

"Don't say that. Besides, I don't think this was some freak accident. I think someone meant to harm you."

He seemed confused. "You do?"

"Uncle, you're a wealthy man. If anyone, including Dawn, wanted to hurt you, Saturday night was a great time to take advantage of you being alone at the ranch."

"You think that Dawn did something to me?"

Candace was adamant. "Well, someone did. You don't remember feeling ill or falling, do you?"

"No, no, I don't. You'd think I would."

"You heard what the doctor said. I'm going to talk to Sam about it, and I want you to take it easy." She patted his hand and was finally able to release it from her grasp.

"I will. Don't you worry about me. You must have so much work to do."

She reached across his frame and hugged his chest. All the tubes had been removed, save for the IV and heart monitor, and he was on his way to healing completely and coming home. "You can't imagine how frightened I was to think you might never recover. I didn't care about anything else. I felt so alone."

Uncle's sturdy arms embraced her as his voice took command of her fears. "I'm not going anywhere any time soon, my dear. You're stuck with me forever, young lady."

"Uncle, we will need to talk more about the letters and what they mean. I didn't really understand them. I never knew about any of the trouble between Aunt Marjorie and Uncle Eric, and I never knew about your fling with her."

His forehead wrinkled in confusion. "My what?"

"Shhhh. Never mind about that right now." She placed two fingers over his lips. "I want you to rest and gain your strength so you can leave this awful place."

Uncle laughed under his breath. "You think I had a fling with Marjorie?"

"It doesn't matter what I think. I'll see you later. Anton and I are going to the ranch and to get a few hours of shut eye, then I'll fill you in on all that's happened while you've been in here."

She turned and walked quickly to the door as Dan laid there

looking puzzled. As Candace emerged from the room, she saw Sam pacing with his hand on his gun as if it was habit while his keys jangled in rhythm. Anton was tapping his foot nervously. They were obviously miffed about being scuttled from the room. The waiting area was less austere than the recovery room but still cold and impersonal.

"I've told him to rest," Candace addressed both men.

"But I wanted to give him his wodka," Anton whined.

She loved the way he said the word naturally using a w sound instead of a v. "We'll see if he can have a little bit when we come back later, don't worry."

"I really need to speak with him, Candace." Sam was insistent.

"I know. And you will, but not now. I can tell you Dawn came to see him on Saturday evening. They had wine together. That's who drank out of the other glass."

"We couldn't match the prints in any criminal database, and that's probably why. That's Dawn Ehrlickson, right?" Sam pulled his notebook from his pocket. "I've questioned her, and she said she was in Denver at the movies that night."

"That's what she told me, too. I don't understand why she would lie about it, but I really can't believe she would hurt my uncle. For years he's been like a surrogate father to her, and he was close to her mom." Candace couldn't say how close. She turned to Anton and leaned against him for support. His face was stern as he put his arm around her frame.

"Well, we'll see. I'm going to look into her alibi and question her more. Her lie puts her as my number one suspect. Unfortunately, because your uncle can't remember the attack, it doesn't clear Jesse's son, but it doesn't incriminate him further."

Candace responded, "We'll be back around noon. I hope you have some more information by then."

Sam crossed his arms. "It's important you don't talk with your friend or anyone else about his recovery or what was said about the matter. Give me some time to investigate."

Candace's mind was running wild. "Okay, although I really want to call her and find out why she lied."

The sheriff shook his head. "Right now, it's best if we keep it just between us and the doctor. I told her not to update his official condition yet so no one knows he's awake."

Anton spoke up, "Do you think we should hire someone to protect him?"

"That's already handled. I've got first watch." Sam removed his hat from his head and pulled up a nearby chair from the nurse's desk.

Candace smiled. "Thank you so much. I sure hope he can get some of his memory back."

"Either way, I'm going to need to take a full statement from him."

"I know."

CHAPTER 24

Another ride to the ranch on the long desert highway. At least this time she didn't need to wrestle with feelings of loss and desperation. For the first time this week she wasn't filled with worry.

Anton's car was as silent as a tomb. Although there was much to say, there was even more to think about. When they reached their destination, rest was the last thing on their minds. Wired from the event, and the ride down to Gallegos, they both needed some time to unwind.

Candace was the first to break the silence. "I suppose I shouldn't be shocked Dawn lied since it seems she kept other stuff from me."

"CJ, I am really, really sorry. I was glad she didn't say anything about the other night, and I wanted to tell you right away, but everything else was happening."

This was not the conversation she wanted to have. "I suppose everything's going to come out now."

"Does it have to?" Anton asked, kneeling to pet Lance.

"Well, she's going to be questioned. How do I tell the sheriff she is less than forthcoming, and I don't trust her, without telling him what else happened?" Candace frowned.

"Maybe she'll just tell him the truth about Saturday night." Anton looked up at her. "Do you think she hurt Dan?"

"I have no clue. It kills me that I can't call her and find out what's going on," she said.

Anton asked. "Why did Dawn come down here in the first place?"

"Something about all those letters." She motioned to the dining room table.

"What's in them?"

Candace explained what she'd read and what she thought it all meant but was sure there was more to the situation than met the eye. "Dawn must have known the letters were there and didn't want Uncle to read them. But why?"

~

The familiar aroma of bacon and fresh pressed coffee pulled Candace into an upright position.

The eastern sunrise shone through the wood shades, making the leather couch glow like honey. Its sheen was almost wet in appearance. A blanket covered with woodland creatures big and small set against a snow drenched mountain and blue sky covered her lap. It was one of Uncle's favorites. The grandfather clock in the corner said 10:20. Five hours sleep was nothing to sneeze at these days. She and Anton had gone through the contents of the boxes again before they fell asleep on the couches.

The clatter of dishes further seduced her growling stomach. Her bare feet padding against the wood flooring, Candace quietly pressed open the large wooden door to maintain the element of surprise. She was taken aback to find a bare-to-the-waist male figure standing at the large commercial grade stove. Honed shoulder muscles flexed as he worked, wearing nothing but jeans slung low from his waistline. His entire back gleamed like a bronze satin sheet. It wasn't Jesse cooking breakfast as she'd thought, it was Anton. His dark hair was tousled from bothered sleep. He was deftly balancing several plates on his hand and arm as he filled them. The yield from wrought iron pots and pans was enough to feed an army.

"Good morning," she spoke as she leaned against the door frame, surveying him from a distance.

The kitchen had been her favorite room in the house since she could remember. Bright and colorful Mexican tiles covered the floor, backsplash and countertops. The sturdy stainless-steel equipment gleamed. The space was equipped with a six-burner stove and side by side refrigerators and freezers which usually stored enough food for a small country club. Sunshine streamed through the wall of windows that overlooked the northern expanse of the ranch with its buildings, water tower and windmills. All of it looking a bit more cheerful than the day before.

"Ah, *Доброе утро*. Good morning. I was hoping you would wake on your own. How did you sleep?"

Candace yawned, putting her hand to her mouth. "Okay. I thought you were Jesse."

"Sorry to disappoint." He smiled.

"How could I be disappointed finding a half-naked man cooking in my kitchen?" She grinned. "Is Jesse here?"

"No. I have not seen her. Riley came by with some fresh eggs but that is all. I told him about Dan but asked him to keep it to himself. He was very happy and said he was going home for a while, but he'd come back to check on everything and feed Lance."

"Thanks for updating him. How long have you been awake?" she said.

"Almost an hour."

"I'd really like to talk to Jesse. Wow. That sure smells good." she said nodding toward the stove. He always managed to rival any menu she could put together and create it on the fly.

"I'm sure it does." He winked and made his way over to the counter, placing several small dishes in front of her. Canadian and regular smoked bacon with scrambled eggs Florentine, and crispy home fries were on a cobalt-blue pottery platter. Cantaloupe cubes and whole fresh figs drizzled with honey filled a mustard yellow bowl. A small tower of seven-grain bread accompanied them.

Candace considered the spread before her, popped a fig in her mouth with one hand while retrieving a slice of crispy bacon in the other. "Thanks, this is awesome."

"No problem." He walked back to the stove, grabbed the coffee pot and creamer and poured a cup for each of them. He finally joined her with a set of plates for himself. A carafe of orange juice and bowls of butter and jam were already in place in front of them along with bold print napkins. He wolfed down a forkful of eggs and fries and took a swig of juice before their eyes met. He smiled. A small piece of spinach dangled from the corner of his mouth. Candace would have automatically used her thumb to remove it, but after what had transpired with Dawn, she just pointed to it.

The food was delicious but more than her sense of taste was piqued as his forearm rubbed against hers. She felt the hair on her own arm tickle and her face flush. She quickly and purposefully moved her arm away and stiffened. "I guess I'll head back to the hospital after breakfast. Tripp and his father are supposed to be coming by, and there's no telling who else will decide to visit."

"I forgot they were coming." He commented but continued to eat like a ravenous animal. Neither had eaten since before the fundraiser.

"Tripp works with his dad now. I stopped by their office on my way to the fundraiser, but he doesn't even know Uncle woke up."

"Are you planning to call Dawn?" he asked.

Candace ate one more bite. "I want to, but I promised Sam I wouldn't."

He gulped some coffee. "What do you think she will say about the letters? After what we read last night, it sounds like she might have a reason to hurt Dan."

"I know, Uncle said Dawn would be angry I read them, but it's all in the past and hardly something she needs to be embarrassed or angry about. In fact, I have more to be angry about than she ever will!" She looked up from her dish and gave him an even stare.

"Candace, I don't blame you for being angry with her and with me. What happened was a stupid mistake. Dawn does not mean anything to me."

"I didn't think so." She swept her plate up off the counter and into the sink. "I don't know how to feel, Anton."

He watched her as she began to systematically put away the leftover food and clean up the remaining dishes. "I will get that. You need to get ready. I guess I will just head back to Denver when I am done," he said.

She was beginning to really hate the influence Dawn was exerting over them. Their interaction was uncomfortable to say the least. "You're not coming to visit him?"

He made his way around the counter and took her hands in his. "Maybe I will go over, but I will not stay long. You have enough on your mind right now."

It was obvious he didn't want to run into Tripp or Dawn. "Okay, I'll try to make it back to Denver tonight."

She felt the pause and a hesitance in the air between them.

Without shoes, her face was at his chest height. Her eyes couldn't help but scan his smooth pecs and ample shoulders on their way up to meet his. They had been close before, elbow to elbow, bodies bumping against each other in a kitchen but never quite like this. He ran both hands through his hair, while every muscle flexed, then he placed them on her shoulders. One of his fingertips found the bottom of her chin, tilted it up to plant a careful kiss on her nose, then he cradled her face in his palms.

"We'll get through this. All of this," he said in a tender tone.

"I hope so." She could feel her lashes moist with tears and carefully pulled away to hide her reaction and left the kitchen without another word.

CHAPTER 25

Neither Anton nor Dawn showed up at the hospital, but it was still a busy day. It astounded Candace she actually felt pangs of jealousy and worse yet, suspicion. Were they together? No, that was simply ridiculous. She admonished herself.

Tripp and Harry came by to discover Uncle carrying on a conversation with Candace about eating Jell-O. She had to swear that the kind he would be required to eat once leaving the hospital was that found in shots containing vodka.

Dan was pleased to find out that the two could visit with him under the guise of legal counsel. Anton had brought a nice bottle of Russia's finest as a gift and Dan was anxious to break it out, but the doctor had left strict directives to the contrary, and even Harry advised him, in true lawyer admonishment.

Dan pretended to be annoyed. "I guess you know who your friends are where vodka is concerned."

"I don't think you need anything to alter your state of consciousness right now, Danno." Harry teased, "We hope to get your memory back to normal, not aid its state of confusion."

"Okay, okay, but you need to come by and have a drink with

me when we do crack it open. It's been far too long since we've tipped back a few."

Harry raised a shaggy eyebrow. "Agreed. Hey, I heard your former heartthrob stopped by to see you. Looking to collect on the life insurance?"

"She did?" His eyes darted to Candace.

"I hadn't told him yet, Harry," Candace interjected. "Yes, Genevieve came to visit you."

Dan answered lightly, "Really? How is the old gal?"

"What old gal?" Tripp entered the conversation. "Full disclosure, man."

"I didn't recognize her, and she only deduced who I was. She asked me about your will and insurance policy. She told me to ask Harry about it."

Dan winked at Harry. "Still as money hungry as ever, huh?"

"Maybe she came by to finish you off?" asked Tripp.

"Nah, she wouldn't know where to begin. Did she say anything else? Leave a note?" Dan asked with unusual curiosity.

Candace answered, "No, no, she didn't but she said she was staying in town and would come back. She came the next day, but I wasn't here. I don't know where she's staying."

"Hmmmm." Dan groaned in thought.

Candace was sure there was a world of information hidden behind that response.

He shifted in his bed. "Who else came by? I'm sorry I missed the party."

She responded, "A couple of your brokers. I have their business cards, and the nurses said some woman who didn't leave her name. I suppose it could have been Aunt Marj. She came by another time. Oh, Dawn and me and Jesse, of course."

"A mystery woman? You been holding out on me, bud?" Harry accused.

After that revelation, Tripp motioned for Candace to leave the room with him. They stepped into the hall. "He looks good. What did he say about his attacker?"

"Nothing. I mean, he has absolutely no memory of what happened."

"That's often the case with head trauma." He took her by the arm and led her down the hall. "So, who do you think the woman was that came by?"

"I haven't a clue. I figured she'd come back or call, but I haven't heard anything. That's not the important part of all this though."

"What do you mean?" Tripp sat next to her in the visitor's seating area.

Candace filled him in on the discussion she had with Uncle in the wee hours after his waking and the news that Dawn had been at the ranch at the time of the attack and had never let on. The two agreed it was more than just a little incriminating.

Tripp volunteered to speak to the Sheriff's office and get to the bottom of the whole story. "I spoke with the Sheriff yesterday afternoon after you left my office. What do you know about your partner's whereabouts around the time of the attack?" Tripp was frowning with concern now.

"My partner? You mean Anton?"

"Do you have another?" He winked, ever the attorney at heart. "Sam was zeroing in on the fact your partner might have had a financial reason for hurting your uncle."

"That's absurd. I told him Anton would never hurt Uncle in a million years. You called Sam?" She never expected him to react that quickly.

Tripp rubbed her arm reassuringly. "Yes, I did. You may be right, but he had information, and he confirmed they were looking at you too. I'm relieved that spotlight has been aimed in a different direction now because it could get messy."

"That's crazy. First of all, Anton was with me the entire day and evening catering a wedding in Evergreen. We were both there when Uncle called."

"Hey, don't shoot the messenger. I wasn't accusing you or anyone else. Just wanted you to know what he said." He reached out and took her hand. "What time did you and Anton get to the reception?"

She enjoyed the security she felt with her hand in his grasp. "I'm not sure. I took my car, and he took the van. It would have been sometime before six, why?"

"No reason in particular. Just creating a timeline."

"Anyway, Uncle was hurt before midnight. I was on the phone with him when it happened, and Anton was right there with me." She was firm.

After going over the points they both wanted covered with Dawn and questions they had for the authorities, they walked shoulder to shoulder back to the room. Tripp advised that Dawn should probably get an attorney fast and promised Candace he would move toward getting Pedro released as soon as possible.

Tripp quietly filled his father in about Dawn's possible complicity in the attack and went on to question Dan about it. Candace couldn't help but be impressed by how precise and thorough he was. Serious but kind, he coaxed answers about specifics from Dan that she would never even think of asking. Harry spoke up now and again, adding his two cents. They seemed to take a good cop, bad cop stance on the entire subject with Tripp being more suspicious and Harry willing to let things slide only to come back with some very direct questions.

Harry squinted as if to zero in on the topic. "What exactly was your relationship with Marjorie?"

Dan said matter-of-factly, "We were never more than friends."

"But the letters seemed to indicate more. She said you were her rock." Candace spoke up. "She mentioned giving in to the Kane magic."

"Well, I suppose I was her rock." Uncle drew in one of his customary long breaths. "But that was all I was. Candace, your aunt Marjorie was in love with your father and had been since before you were born."

"What? Daddy would never," she spoke from a panicky little girl place.

"No, no, my dear," he commanded calm with his tone. "Your father wasn't even aware. In fact, he was so in love with your mother, and so busy with work, I don't think he ever would have noticed."

Tripp and Harry watched and listened as the story unfolded.

"Marjorie was a lonely, unhappy woman, and over time she became very attached to Brad. He was around when Eric never was, and she began to imagine a life with him."

"Did Mom know?" She winced.

"No, Marj confessed her feelings for him to me and only me. I tried to make her see they would never be reciprocated, but she was and is a very determined woman. Just before your parents were killed, she made the decision to tell your father. But I don't think she ever had the chance."

Candace wondered if Dawn had any idea. Dawn had read all the letters way back then and hid them. Did she keep them secret because of her mom's feelings or because she thought her mom and Uncle Dan were having an affair? This whole thing was beginning to unravel, and not in Dawn's favor.

It was nearly four in the afternoon when Candace walked Harry and Tripp to the elevator. Jesse had arrived around two and had spent time fussing over her boss and profusely apologizing for her absence the night he was injured. Like a well-worn glove, their conversation was smooth and an easy fit. A little alone time with Jesse would bring Uncle a sense of normalcy.

Swimming in a plethora of facts and suspicions when Sheriff Sam descended on the waiting room to discuss what his investigation had revealed to date, her head was beginning to pound. The good news was that Pedro was no longer considered a suspect and Candace couldn't wait to tell Jesse. The bad news was that Dawn was turning out to be enemy number one and was still among the missing. Candace admitted she hadn't heard from Dawn since last night, and that was highly unusual. They hadn't spoken since the fundraiser. She called Anton, but he hadn't heard from her either.

Harry gave Candace a reassuring bear hug as he entered the elevator. There was an unspoken father-son exchange that passed between he and Tripp just before Harry released the door. Tripp and Candace stood in silence, watching it close.

Tripp broke the quiet with his voice. "I was wondering if you'd like to have dinner tonight. I know it's been quite a day. I thought you might need a little break." Tripp was as cool, crisp and pressed as when he arrived hours ago. She felt like one of the dozens of withering plants just outside her uncle's room. Not even a shower could resurrect her.

"That's such a nice thought, but I'm really beat, Tripp. How 'bout a rain check?"

He grinned at her. "A rain check is fine, but I hate to just leave you all alone with so many unanswered questions."

She felt small. Like the innocent school girl he first met. But she wasn't. She was much stronger than that girl who ran from the best relationship she would ever have. Life was strange.

"I appreciate that, but honestly I'll just grab a bite to eat with Uncle, spend a little time with Jesse, go back to the ranch and go to bed."

"Okay." He hit the call button for the elevator then turned and enfolded her in his arms, swaying as if they were dancing. She felt as she had in his office, off balance, uncertain. He held onto her as he drew back and tentatively planted a soft kiss on her cheek. She sensed people watching but was not willing to pull away. Memories came flooding in. Good memories. Did he feel them too? A moment later he disappeared through the doors.

∾

When the doctor made her final rounds, Uncle Dan was in a great mood. Candace was too. It might have been a residual feeling from the hug at the elevator or the general feeling of levity in the room, but Candace could have sworn Uncle Dan and the doctor were flirting through most of her consultation.

The same woman who watched over him in his coma and at his bedside when he woke, was about ten years his junior. Without the green surgical cap, her shoulder-length auburn hair was secured with a single elastic band. She wore a conservative amount of makeup, save her pink lip gloss. They framed an uneven but toothy smile. She wore a skirt under her white coat, and to Candace's surprise, when she sat down next to his bed, she thought she caught Uncle checking out the doctor's shapely legs.

In conversation, she admitted to being single and a native to Gallegos. She lived about 30 minutes from the hospital in the direction of the ranch. The doctor shared she had attended more than one Double K event in the past and had some wonderful memories there. As she talked and laughed, her long, narrow nose wrinkled and sharpened to a point. Her umber complexion was highlighted by plum blush-dusted cheek bones, which accented her deep-set dark eyes hidden behind thin metal-rimmed glasses. Candace could see what Dan saw in her.

Could Uncle Dan really be interested? Candace had always envisioned Jesse and Uncle together someday, but stranger things happen. She watched as Jesse looked on. It was funny thinking of him with another woman, but funnier still, thinking of him with the likes of Genevieve. Thank god that relationship never got off the ground.

Candace took off for the ranch, leaving Jesse with her uncle. Windows open and music blaring to stay awake, it turned into quite a busy drive. Phone calls were placed to at least a dozen interested parties. Friends and former business associates were anxious to know his condition. She even tried to reach Dawn, although she didn't know what to say. Catching Anton at the office, she wondered how she could ever doubt him. He was the hardest working, most diligent and trustworthy man she knew aside from her uncle, and well, Tripp.

Anton was using a computer program that hacked into Dan's cell phone. He told her nothing had come up except the letters PLE, corresponded with the numbers Dan had last dialed on his phone. They discussed the possibility that he might have been trying to type 'please help' to text to Candace.

"I wish he could remember something, anything about that night," she told him. "Now it makes total sense why Dawn was able to show up at the hospital at 4:00 a.m. She had been just up the road at the ranch. I wonder where she was when I was sitting there alone, freaking out."

They agreed to keep focused on Dawn.

The front gates of the Double K were a welcome sight. As Candace drove onto the property, she sensed something different about it. She discovered the reason in just a few feet. Either Jesse or Riley must have been there, because the courtyard was alive with color and activity. The sun would set in about an hour but she could see that the fountain had been filled and set in motion.

She walked past the trees and bushes with birds dive bombing the full feeders on the edge of the front porch. The planter boxes had been emptied and refilled with perennial flowers and blooming cactus. It was like a scene from a Disney movie. The entire garden had come to life with Uncle waking up.

"What do you think, Miss Candace?" Riley, hatless, red faced and dirty walked toward her.

"I love it!"

He ran his fingers through his hair. "I thought we'd get ready for Mr. Dan's return home."

"Riley, what would we...he...do without you?"

"I hope you'll never find out."

"Me too. Never ever." She gave the man a quick hug, careful

not to share too much flora and fauna from the garden, then returned to the house. She stopped just shy of the door and asked, "Did Jesse call?"

"Yes. She's on her way to El Paso. It seems her son is off the hook about Mr. Dan's attack and was given permission to leave town, so she and her husband are taking him out to celebrate."

"Awesome. This has been one great day, hasn't it? Why don't you go on home? I'll be fine here tonight."

"Yes ma'am. I'll see you tomorrow."

CHAPTER 26

Lance was barking when Candace exited her much desired shower. She wrapped herself in the awaiting robe and sprinted to look out the window. She had been drenched in the hot, steamy water for so long t night had fallen. A quick glance showed nothing because the lights in the courtyard weren't on, not even the spotlights on the trees. Maybe Riley forgot to set the timer.

"It's okay, boy," she said scratching the top of his head. Lance was very convincing. He sensed something.

"What is it boy? Is someone out there, or do you want to chase prairie dogs?"

Lance barked with renewed fervor, almost threatening.

Candace flipped on the porch light and went into the kitchen to check the side patio. The great bay windows revealed nothing. She shivered. The desert nights were always chilly. The sun setting caused a good twenty to thirty drop in temperature overnight, and she was still dripping underneath her robe.

"I can't let you out, buddy." She didn't dare since she was alone, and she wasn't as good at delivering proper commands like Uncle. Distracted, Lance might not come back inside. He began to pace back and forth, running from room to room and jumping at the front door. Candace froze. She had never seen him like this.

She peeked out the front window again and stood on her tiptoes at the door to see through the peephole. Nothing. This was not funny.

"Quiet down!" she snapped at Lance, overwhelmed by his frantic reaction to nothing she could see.

Lance, honoring her command jumped, gnawed at the front door knob growling and shaking his head in a tearing fashion. She watched, terrified at what his teeth and that level of vehemence could do to a person. At the same time, she was relieved she had him as her guardian and not-so-secret weapon.

Weapon!

She darted to Uncle's office where his special cabinet was loaded with guns and ammunition. The hollow sound of loud thumps stopped her dead in her tracks.

"Who's there?" she yelled but wanted to cry. She held her ground and her breath. Was someone knocking or was it just the shutters in the wind?

She grabbed the first handgun she found and thrashed through the ammunition. Her hand shook as she loaded the heavy pistol. One...two...three bullets. The pounding stopped her again. It was coming from the direction of the front door.

She slowly approached. "Hello? Who is it?"

She held the revolver with both hands, her arms the consistency of aspic.

A voice called out, "It's me, Tripp."

"What? Oh my God!"

Lance ceased barking and cocked his head toward Candace to confirm she knew the caller's identity. She dropped the gun to her side and staggered toward the door, straightening the fit of her robe.

She opened the door prepared to decapitate him with words,

but there he stood, pizza and a bottle of red wine in hand. "What are you doing here?"

"I parked out near the gate and couldn't see my way in the dark, and then I thought your horse here was going to eat me."

She stepped back to allow him entrance, but he hesitated, clearly convinced canine dissection was imminent. Candace burst out laughing. Not a normal guffaw but uncontrollable laughter nearing hysteria. It took a moment, but Tripp joined her and they both collapsed against the door. Lance stood on guard but perplexed.

"I was about to shoot whoever it was until you answered me." She spat out holding her sides.

"I wasn't sure what to do. I really thought that dog was going to come through the door."

She scratched the animal's head. "That dog is Lance. Sir Lancelot, Uncle's dog. Lance, meet Tripp."

"Hi Lance. I'd shake your paw, but my hands are a little full right now." He lifted the pizza box.

"Oh, I'm sorry. Come in and put all that stuff down."

Tripp made his way to the coffee table in the family room. "So, this is the mate to the dog that was killed?"

"Actually, they were brothers from the same litter."

"Hey, boy. Thanks for guarding our girl. I'm okay. I promise not to bite you if you don't bite me."

"I didn't know you were coming out here and it's pretty desolate. You're lucky I didn't shoot you." They both looked down at the gun still in her hand.

"I'd say we're both lucky. Ahhh, let me take that off your hands. I think I'd feel safer." He grinned and liberated it from her grasp. "I'm so sorry. I tried to call your cell, but you didn't answer. I wanted to bring you something to eat and check in on you after all. I guess I really screwed that one up."

"I was in the shower. A really long shower and didn't hear the phone. If that pizza has anchovies or black olives then you're forgiven."

"It has both, black olives *and* anchovies with extra cheese." He dropped it on the side table.

She was touched. "You remembered."

"How could anyone forget a pizza like that?"

She saw his eyes assessing her robe. Was he really checking her out?

"Wow. This place is great." He scanned the room, nodding. "I love how it feels here."

"Me too. Ready to eat?" he asked.

"Umm, I guess so. Maybe I should change first."

"Don't bother," he said, raising both palms up beside his ears. "I promise to mind my manners. Just stay comfortable."

"Thanks." She went into the kitchen and popped right back with a couple of plates, two wine glasses and a wine opener with her pinkie.

"I wasn't sure if you were still a wine girl. I could have brought beer."

She smiled. "Once a wine girl, always a wine girl. But *you* could have had beer."

He sat on the couch. His legs relaxed as she curled hers underneath her body to sit at his level. Her manicured toes peeked out from underneath her robe. She dished up the pizza from the coffee table while he opened the wine with flourish and poured a sip to sample.

"Adequate, considering the liquor store inventory." He winked. "You probably have something much better here."

"It's fine." She felt as if his eyes were devouring her instead of the pizza when he sat back and proposed a simple toast. "To Dan and the circumstances that brought us into each other's lives again."

She smiled, uncertain but clinked his glass politely.

Candace couldn't wait to take a great big bite of the pizza. She never knew anyone else who liked this exact combination of toppings, except her Dad.

Tripp wolfed down one piece in three bites leaving some of the greasy marinara sauce dribbled down his chin. She grinned.

"What?"

"You've got sauce on your chin. I think you forgot to get napkins."

"I'll go get some or you could kiss it off." He leaned in and produced his lower lip.

She tried not to laugh as he pursed them. She kissed carefully at the spot then proceeded to "clean" his chin, talking between kisses, "Feel...free...to object, counselor." She was feeling bold, more confident than she did years ago.

"Overruled," he purred and pulled her onto her knees and across his body in one swift movement. His lips caught her mouth. He separated hers with his tongue and took his time.

As if tasting delicious vintage, he moved his tongue back and forth and up and down. She followed his seemingly effortless pattern and gave into him completely. They kissed as they had the first time so many years ago. The passion, tingling sensations, the unbridled emotion that she felt then came rushing back.

He leaned back to end the kiss only to have it continue onto her neck creating a path down the center of her robe. His tongue touched her skin, and for a moment, she couldn't catch her breath. She felt him wanting her, and she wanted him to take her in his arms, removing all the fear and stress of the past week, replacing it with excitement and satisfaction. She was on fire within.

"I know I promised to behave, but god I want you." He cleared his throat and looked up. He was doing his best to communicate with words.

"I know," she whispered. "Honestly, I don't want it to be lost in everything else, not after all this time."

"It's okay, just relax." he said, moving the folded collar of the robe to the right a few inches with his teeth. He placed his mouth over her breast. He sucked, licked, then pulled back to look again as if he wanted to clearly see the object of his desire. Had he thought about this moment for years like she had? Had he spent too many nights in the company of his law books instead of with her, thinking about what might have been?

Candace arched her back, pushing her chest toward his mouth. He accepted the invitation gladly and slid his lower body onto the couch over hers. The room was dark with the exception of the glow from the porchlight through the windows. She felt swallowed up by his mass.

Her robe had fallen open, and his hand explored her delicately. She was happy he was keeping his promise, looking and touching without removing his clothes and culminating the moment. Tonight was not the night. She felt special, precious. This was heaven. They kissed for what seemed hours and held each other so close they were nearly one.

The house phone broke the quiet with a shrill ring, and seconds later her cell phone rang and vibrated, rattling against the coffee table. Tripp jumped up and grabbed it, handing it to her.

"Hello?" Candace said, pleased to see Tripp beside her. What time was it?

"Hello, Ms. Kane?"

"Yes."

"This is Dr. Melendez. Your uncle has suffered a cardiac arrest." Her voice cracked uncharacteristically. "Luckily, we did not remove his monitor today and we were able to revive him in time, but I think you might want to come to the hospital."

She swallowed a sob. "What? No! Oh my God."

Tripp was obviously alerted by her tone. "What is it? What's wrong?"

"Yes, okay, I will. I will be right there." She disconnected without a goodbye.

Tripp sat on the edge of the couch. She disintegrated before him. Distraught. Hysterical. "Uncle...Uncle had a heart attack."

"Oh, Candace, I'm so sorry. What did they say? Is he alive?"

"Yes, they revived him, but I need to go to him. I don't know what's happening."

"Let's go." Tripp was immediately in charge. He gathered up the pizza and wine remnants, transporting them into the kitchen, and then led her into her bedroom. He asked for directions in finding the clothing she wanted to wear. Thankfully she had laid out her jeans and shirt for after her shower, and he managed to find a bra and panties in her top drawer.

He rested his hand on her arm. "I'll pull the car up. You get dressed. Don't worry, I'll get your purse and phone."

She thanked God then and there for Tripp.

They were in the car and on the way in no time flat, and Tripp began making phone calls from Candace's cell. His first call was to Anton. He filled him in and told him where they were headed. His second call was to Jesse. He politely reminded her who he was, how he knew Dan, and as gently as he could, broke the news. Then, he called his dad.

He must have been driving his Mercedes over 100 miles an hour but she didn't care. She was curled up in a ball sobbing. She surrendered to the shock and hopelessness she had felt all along. Would anything ever be right again? Candace prayed to God, her mother and the stars in the sky. Tripp held her hand tightly.

By the time they reached the curved driveway in front of the hospital, Candace had composed herself enough to run a brush through her hair. They were a disheveled pair, Tripp with his shirt tails out of his pants and buttons undone at the neck, and she with her tear-streaked, red and swollen face. She looked at him and smiled tenderly. At this moment in time, he was her hero.

They ran through the lobby, down the corridor, into the elevator and down the third-floor hallway in unison.

CHAPTER 27

Nurses and doctors gathered around Uncle Dan's room once again, producing an odd sensation of *déjà vu* for Candace. Some exhibited stern and concerned expressions while others buried their heads in note taking. Dr. Melendez made her way from across the room to Candace's side.

"Doctor?" Candace's voice was trembling.

The doctor led her by the elbow into an adjoining room. "He's out of the woods for now and resting comfortably, but it was a close call. We're in the process of running further tests, but I believe he'll be fine. We've taken the precaution of calling the sheriff's office."

"Thank God," Candace mumbled aloud, but inside her heart leapt, silently praising God for answering her prayers. She motioned to Tripp to join them.

"Wait, the sheriff's office? What does the Sheriff have to do with a heart attack?"

"Ms. Kane," the doctor began, giving a leveled stare at Tripp.

"Oh please, just call me Candace."

Dr. Melendez greeted her request with an accepting nod. "Candace, the consensus of opinion among the doctors is that your uncle may have been poisoned. We are doing tests, blood work and taking every precaution."

"Poisoned–what the hell?" She wrapped her arms around her waist. Tripp steadied her.

The doctor continued, "Please understand we haven't confirmed anything, but your uncle took an unexpected, and frankly inexplicable turn for the worse. He coded for no evident reason. His symptoms are similar to those with poisoning or overdose. Hospital security has been placed on your uncle's door while we wait for a deputy. For now, visitors are limited to only you and Jesse."

"Yes, right. That would be right. Did you speak with Sheriff Solodad?"

"Yes, I did. His name and number are on our records in case of an emergency. I told him our suspicions."

As if he'd heard them talking, the sheriff came bounding down the hall. "CJ, I'm glad you're here. I'm so sorry. Doctor, how is the patient doing?" He motioned to one of his deputies to cover the door.

The doctor answered, "I'm just very grateful that the heart monitor alerted us in time to save him."

"Any news on the bloodwork?" Sam was definitely handling himself in a distanced and professional manner. Uncle would be proud of him, although right now he was talking about the man like he was some sort of stranger, a piece of meat lying in that horrible hospital bed.

"Not as yet, but it should be anytime now. I will find you just as soon as I know anything." She began to step away.

"Doctor," Tripp chimed in. "Would you please take my card and be sure my office is contacted with any and all updates on Mr. Kane's condition? My law firm currently holds his power of attorney."

"Certainly, sir" she said, making note in the chart she held.

Candace shot Tripp a surprised look but said nothing. Tripp and his father held his power of attorney? This was news to her.

The sheriff spoke up, "Candace, tonight moves us into a new phase of the investigation. If the doctor is right, following the other night, I'd say someone definitely has it in for Dan."

"It certainly appears that way," Candace said.

"If he's right, you could be in danger too." Tripp added.

Candace was numb and just nodded in silence. She couldn't shake that vulnerable feeling earlier at the ranch tonight. Thank goodness it had been Tripp who showed up at the door.

"My advice is lay low for now," Sam said. "You might want to go back to your office in Denver or stay at the ranch with a guard 24/7 'til we catch this guy."

The doctor was visibly concerned. "I can have them set up a room directly across the hall from your uncle for you, Ms. Kane."

"Or, she can stay at my place," Tripp announced.

"Thank you, doctor, but I'll be fine either at the ranch or my office," Candace carefully ignored Tripp's suggestion. "Just please take good care of him."

The doctor patted Candace's arm and both she and the sheriff bowed out of the conversation, heads together in serious conversation.

"You can stay at my place, you know. I have plenty of room and a very good security system. No one will think to look for you there." Tripp reassured her.

"No, I don't want to be that far away from him. I don't want to go back to Denver either. I need to find out what's going on and get more help. I'll call a couple of the hands at the ranch and have them stay the night. They know the place even in pitch black, and with Lance there, I'll be safe."

"Then I'll stay with you. I can take one of the guest rooms."

"That would be nice. You don't need to."

"But I want to." He stepped closer and hugged her shoulders with his ample arm.

"Okay." She looked up at him and smiled, knowing how comfortable that would make her feel. She hadn't felt that at ease or secure since before Uncle was attacked.

He planted a kiss on her forehead. "Candace, no matter what happens, I'm here for you."

"Who do you think tried to kill Uncle?"

"I wouldn't put it past that old girlfriend of his. She does have an axe to grind. I shouldn't tell you this, but she *is* in that old will he executed."

Candace was surprised by this new knowledge as well. She added, "But then, there's Dawn. Why do you suppose she lied about her whereabouts, and where has she been?"

He raised his brow. "That will be the hot topic of conversation when the sheriff finds her."

"I want to go in and be with him." She felt like a little girl once again.

Tripp slid the heavy glass door open with one hand and allowed her some privacy with Dan.

CHAPTER 28

Facing yet another event without his partner, and determined to be by her side, Anton was up for hours after Tripp's call, planning and reviewing everything about the upcoming brunch. In just a short while, 200 guests would fill the Butterfly World in Denver, a unique venue that allowed brides to set free butterflies to flit through the rooms, creating a natural ambiance that made a photographer's job all the more interesting.

Barely able to keep focused, his brain kept whirling with thoughts of Candace, Dan and wondering what Dawn could be up to. He called her twice after hearing about Dan's heart failure from Tripp of all people, but there had been no response. How did that guy end up being with her tonight? Candace had clearly told Anton he had left this afternoon. Was Candace keeping the truth from him? Would she do that on purpose?

Another shot of vodka would relax him, but it wouldn't make him think any more clearly, and he had to keep his head in the game.

Calling Cameron in the wee hours was unusual but not unheard of. "This will be the perfect opportunity for you and

Zach to step up and run an event without us," he explained, telling Cam what had transpired. "I just can't stand to think of her going through this alone."

He knew Cam would be eager to orchestrate an event from the kitchen and had equal confidence that Zach could handle the front of the house. Cam would take Anton's place executing all the dishes on the menu and managing the kitchen staff. Zach could easily step into Candace's shoes, managing the serving staff, setting up the dining room tables and buffet and making sure everything was served on time. A brunch was typically not as labor intensive in the kitchen with many items prepped and baked ahead. A buffet was much easier on the serving staff, although perfection was still demanded.

"Okay, man. Keep your phone handy if I need to call you," Cam said. "Send CJ our best." Anton knew Cameron wouldn't be able to go back and sleep now. He told him to download the menu and head for the kitchen to make sure everything was ready to go.

Cameron was confident. "We got this. Don't worry."

"You better. I need to head down to the hospital and make sure Candace and Dan are okay. Call me for anything."

"You bet."

Anton, in the car heading south, tried Dawn once more. He suspected he might get her at this hour and did. "It's been two days since anyone has heard anything from you," Anton chastised her as if he were a parent and then thought better of it.

"So," she said flippantly.

"So? Candace is worried about you, and what is all this crap about you being at the ranch the night Dan was hurt? Where have you been?"

"What? Who told you that?" Dawn sounded dumbfounded.

In his frustration, he realized he had spoken out of turn and had forgotten the need for secrecy with the police looking for her. Maybe he could get her to turn herself in.

He cleared his throat. "I think Candace told me. She said Dan woke up and told them you had been there. She also told me about some letters."

"She what? Those are personal and certainly none of *your* business." He could hear her seething. She rattled on, "Dan's awake? Why didn't she tell me?"

"If you would return phone calls maybe you'd know. I think you should get in touch with her tonight. Where have you been anyway?"

"I was with Congressman Tethermeyer. We took an overnight trip to Blackhawk. This *is* a free country, remember?"

Of course, Dawn would just take off at a time like this. Blackhawk, Colorado's stepsister to the lavish Las Vegas strip, was tucked in the front mountain range about forty minutes from Denver. It was an easy getaway with much the same attractions but on a smaller scale, gambling at several casinos, food buffets and discounted high-roller suites. It was a favorite hangout for the locals who couldn't spare the time to getaway to Nevada. Did she really go out of town? When did she actually get back?

She continued in a defensive tone, "Look, I didn't say anything about being at the ranch with Dan because I didn't hurt him. He was fine when I left. When I found out he might never wake up, I didn't want to get in trouble with the cops. I was going to tell Candace when I got back."

"Well, your cat is out of the box now, and so is that other little secret."

"You told her? You idiot–it's bag, not box. The cat is out of the bag. Don't try to speak our language if you don't understand it, you fool."

"What did you think I was going to do, keep it a secret and let you use it against me? I know how you operate, Dawn." He tried not to be completely hostile. "I only told her it happened, that's all."

"I'm going down there now. I'll call Candace and let her know. Stay out of this, and keep your mouth shut, do you hear me? Don't tell her anything more than you already have. I know how to handle her, and you don't know anything about me," she practically yelled at him and then hung up.

He pressed the gas pedal to the floor.

CHAPTER 29

Tripp and Candace reached the ranch about two in the morning. Sleep deprived and drained of all the will to walk another step, Candace cringed when she heard Dawn's shrill ringtone break through her jeans. She drew in a deep breath similar to how her Uncle often did. Might he use that pause as a moment to prepare or steel himself as she was now?

"It's Dawn," she told Tripp and clicked on the speaker phone. "Where have you been?" Her plan to act completely calm disappeared.

"I was in Blackhawk with Ronnie. You know how poor the cell reception is there. I didn't know you were trying to reach me. I'm on my way down now. I should be there in a few hours. I never would have gone away if I had known you needed me."

"Needed you? Dawn, I can't begin to tell you everything that has happened, and I don't really want to see you tonight–I mean this morning. This has been one hell of a day."

Dawn's tone was so typically condescending. "You're just mad at me about Anton. I know he told you. Candace, men are just dogs. You need to let me explain. What really hurts is that you'd let Anton come tonight and not me."

"Anton? He's not coming down."

"Oh yes he is! I just spoke with him. I think he's going to see Dan, but I wanted to call you ASAP when I heard he told you about what happened between us. I'm sure what you're thinking is a lot worse than the truth."

"Dawn, I'm not going to discuss it with you or anyone else. It's just not a priority right now." She hit mute. The less Tripp knew about all this the better.

"She and Anton are both on their way down from Denver," she told him.

Tripp said, "Can you get her to come here. We'll call the sheriff."

"Hello? Hello? Did I lose you?" Dawn was calling out.

Candace clicked off mute. "No, I'm here. I just got to the ranch. Why don't you come straight here, and we'll have a chance to talk?" She looked at Tripp with a question in her expression. He nodded his head in agreement.

"Okay...I'm on my way."

Candace gritted her teeth, repulsed by her own plan. She rolled her eyes at Tripp as she told Dawn, "See you soon. Bye."

Candace sat down hard on the couch that just a few hours ago had held such warmth and passion for her and Tripp. It seemed a distant memory now.

After some thought, she said, "I don't want to call the sheriff just yet. I need to talk to Dawn on my own."

"What? Are you kidding?"

"No, I'm dead serious."

He scoffed. "Dead, being the operative word here. She could try to kill you. At the very least she needs to be arrested for the attempted murder of your uncle."

"I know what you're thinking, but I know Dawn better than anyone. Underneath that chilly exterior is a little girl who lived through some of the same stuff I did. I fell apart, but she erected walls." Candace was suddenly very sad. "You should go home anyway. You need a break as much as I do."

"What? I'm not leaving you here to wait for her."

"Yes, you are. We have some very personal things to talk about, and she would resent an audience." Candace wouldn't be too thrilled with Tripp hearing any conversation about Anton either. She stood up and took his hand, leading him to the door.

"Candace, I can't just…"

She cut him off. "Yes, yes you can, and if you care about me you will. I'm not a little girl, Tripp, and I need to handle this by myself. Riley and the guys are on their way, and so is Anton, I guess. It's not that long until sunrise. Now get on the road. I will call you." She placed her hands squarely on his chest.

With that, she gave him a reassuring kiss goodbye. She wished that last night could have been one of the most special nights of her life, but once again, circumstances got in the way.

Tripp looked deeply into her eyes. "Earlier tonight was amazing."

"Yes, it was. You're amazing." She kissed him again and opened the heavy wooden door. She had to practically push him through it and watched until his car was completely out of sight.

CHAPTER 30

It was nearly eight when Candace jumped into her SUV, to catch up with Dawn. Just an hour ago, Dawn had arrived at the ranch, offered an insincere hug, accepted a cup of coffee, and began a seemingly well-rehearsed story about what she'd been up to. The ranch was oddly quiet and the house eerily empty. Their conversation became heated and their voices reverberated. Everything had changed over the last few days.

Candace was confused. "I can't believe you never told me about the letters. You never let on that your mom and dad were having trouble."

Dawn explained, "I was embarrassed and not entirely sure what was going to happen. Dad would never leave Mom, at least not from what I knew. I guess if I hid them and didn't tell anyone, it made it all go away."

Candace had faced Dawn with the particulars just as she and Anton planned when they read the letters yesterday morning. They'd pieced together a timeline, linking Dawn's visit to the hospital that night and the suspicious activity at the ranch with Dawn's vanishing act from Denver with no credible explanation. She certainly hadn't gone to the movies.

Candace finally told Dawn what Uncle had told her. It was Candace's father Brad, not Dan, who had stolen Marjorie's heart. Brad was the reason Marjorie was prepared to leave Dawn's father. Had Brad and Cynthia not gone off the edge of that cliff so many years ago, Dawn might have discovered her mother's plans were in vain and her feelings not even reciprocated.

Standing in the same room where Dan was nearly slain, holding the opened envelopes and red ribbon, Dawn had cried out. "First, his own wife professes love for his best friend, then that bitch from Dan's firm strips him financially," she spat out the words. Her hair disheveled, makeup smeared from crying, and hands shaking, Dawn was less her social climbing self and more like the young teen Candace remembered.

She then stormed out of the door, screaming, "How could she? She was going to just abandon my father? No wonder he took his own life!"

Candace wasn't certain where Dawn was headed. Driving in the direction of the hospital like a bat out of hell, sand spewing from the tires, Dawn swerved. She was obviously reeling from what she and Candace had just discussed. If everything discovered within those boxes of letters was true and her actions last week actually did coincide with Dan's attack, the girl needed serious help.

Candace choked back the tears. If only Dawn's mother and father had stayed together, it might have meant more father-daughter time and no matter what the financial fallout, she knew Dawn would have still worshiped her father. Could it all have been prevented? Was Dawn headed to the hospital to confess to come clean about the betrayal she felt had taken place, and the years she carried hate in her heart? Was she going to fall on her own sword to clear her name and square things with Dan or try to hurt him again?

Candace now wondered about Aunt Marjorie's visit to the

hospital a few days ago. Still following Dawn, she slowed, just long enough to make a call on her cell.

"Hello?" It had been so long since she'd heard her voice.

"Aunt Marj? It's Candace."

"Oh no, Candace. Don't tell me something has happened to your uncle."

"No, he's okay. I didn't mean to frighten you by calling, but I need your help."

"What is it, dear?"

"I'm sorry to be the one to tell you, but Uncle Dan's accident was more than that. Dawn was involved. She didn't mean to hurt him but she did have an argument with Uncle.

"Oh my God. I was afraid something bad would happen between them one day. Dawn has harbored such animosity in her heart toward him. I came to see him the other day, but visiting wasn't allowed. I thought we should both talk to Dawn."

"I'm afraid it's even more serious than that, Aunt Marj. Can you tell me more about what happened back then?"

With Candace still in hot pursuit of Dawn, Marjorie painted a very different picture of the situation. Among the many details she already knew, Aunt Marj shared some she didn't. Her aunt explained that when she confessed her feelings about Brad to her husband Eric, he had made threats and stormed off in a rage.

"We had a horrible fight," she explained. "He said he'd divorce me, take Dawn away from me and find a way to ruin your father. He started acting crazy and said that if he couldn't have me then Brad couldn't either, and he'd kill him if he pursued me. I'm so sorry Candace, we never meant for you to find out any of this. Honestly, after your parent's bodies were discovered, I thought it was put in the past for good."

"Uncle Dan knew about how angry Uncle Eric, er, your husband had been?" Candace asked, beginning to feel even more uncomfortable.

"Yes, I spoke with him about it briefly. God forgive me,

Candace. I wonder to this day if Eric had been capable of hurting your Dad. I was afraid he killed himself because he had a part in it." Marjorie was remorseful.

Candace was numb with realization. Could her parent's accident have somehow been an attack? That wasn't the Uncle Eric she remembered, but if it were true, her mom and dad's death might not have been an accident after all. It might have been murder.

Marjorie explained that it was less than a year after their break up when Eric shot himself. "I don't think it was over the money. You know, the stock market losses, but your uncle thought so. Eric and Dan were both inconsolable about your parents, we all were, and your uncle wouldn't hear of any suspicions involving Eric."

Candace wept when they finished the conversation. She could barely see the road or Dawn's car in the distance, but she was obviously headed for the hospital. Relieved to hear her parents had the strong marriage she always suspected they did, the fact that it ended too soon and so abruptly, made it devastating.

She had a sudden urge to investigate it all, to delve into this heavily guarded past while Dan was still at the hospital, alive and in protective custody. If Uncle Eric, she winced at the reference to their formerly close relationship, had killed her parents, and Dawn was as unstable as she seemed, there was no telling how much danger Uncle could be in right now.

Candace thanked Marjorie and told her it might be a good idea to drive in from Boulder again to see both Dawn and Uncle Dan. Candace promised her that they would find out who was responsible and if it was Dawn, they'd try to help her.

Dialing Anton was both a relief and a strain. She had to tell him their plan worked. That she had confronted Dawn with the letters they had studied with a fine-tooth comb. In the light of day and with maturity, they had revealed to Dawn how wrong she had been.

When he picked up, Candace told him, "I think she's on her way to the hospital. She may try to hurt Uncle for his part in all this. She seems dangerously close to a breakdown."

He assured her, "I'm here at the hospital now. Don't worry. Drive carefully."

"Thanks. Hey, what about the brunch?"

"The boys are getting their first shot at running things by themselves. I wasn't sure if this was going to be the day when it all came to a head, but I called Cam, and he said he and Zach would be fine. Fingers crossed."

She sighed. "I guess it was bound to happen sometime. I feel as if I have abandoned the business."

"No worries, it's all going to come to an end soon. Everything will be back to normal."

"Anton, I spoke with my aunt. She said her husband once threatened to kill my dad." She choked on the words and swallowed her tears.

"Seriously? Does she have proof?"

"No, just his threat. It was after Eric found out about Marj's feelings for my dad."

"Wow, but who's trying to hurt Dan now? Have you called the sheriff?"

"No, I guess I should," she said.

"I would. Don't worry, I'm here."

CHAPTER 31

C andace pulled into the parking lot just behind Dawn. She watched her scurry out of the car and into the hospital. Candace jumped out of her car and ran after her. By the time the elevator doors opened on Dan's floor, she could hear Dawn shouting.

"Just let me go! You can't tell him, he'll never forgive me," Dawn was screaming as Anton was restraining her from entering Dan's room. The nurse staff was blustering about, and she could hear one on the phone to the sheriff. Dawn was hysterical.

Anton clenched Dawn's arm so tight it was turning red.

"Let go, I need to talk to him about the other night when he got hurt and about what's in the letters." She twisted her arm, thrust her knee into Anton's groin and ran into Dan's room. Candace sprinted to Anton's side as he cursed, bent in half, swearing. "Son of a bitch."

Candace followed her into Dan's room where Dawn collapsed into the chair beside Uncle's bed, sobbing. She looked like a shriveled spider, recoiled from a glancing blow.

Dan rolled over. "What's going on?"

"We know who hurt you, Uncle, and who's been at the center of this entire thing," Candace blurted.

"Well, spit it out," he said, glancing at Dawn. "Or maybe you're not the one to tell me."

"No, I might as well," Dawn spoke into her shaking hands. Peeking out from between her fingers she asked him, "You can't believe I'd really do anything to hurt you, can you?"

"I know you were pretty angry with me the other night, about me keeping the letters, but honestly Dawn, I don't remember what happened after that."

"I ran out the door and left. The first I heard you were really hurt was when Anton told me. I turned back and went straight to the hospital."

Anton came into the room. "Come on Dawn, he was hit over the head with something–probably the fireplace poker. Did you hit him with it? You need to come clean."

Dawn retorted quickly, "No! Are you crazy? Why would I try to kill him? I was angry is all."

"If not you, then who? The hospital has proof someone tried to kill him again, and no one could reach you," Anton said accusingly.

"They what?" Dan seemed shocked by Anton's statement.

Dawn looked at him sincerely. "Dan, you can't think I would try to kill you. I was in Blackhawk with a client."

Uncle Dan said, "I don't know what to think, young lady, but it will all be sorted out, I'm sure. If you are really innocent then you don't need to worry, but we need to talk about those letters, and I would like to talk to your mother."

Sheriff Sam entered the room.

"Sam, I'm glad you're here," Candace sighed the words. "Dawn swears she didn't attack Dan, only that she only pushed him, and he was fine when she left the ranch. Last night she was supposedly in Blackhawk."

The sheriff was already pulling a crying Dawn to her feet with one hand and reaching for his handcuffs with the other. "Ms. Erhlickson, you are under arrest for attempted murder. You have the right to remain silent. Anything you say can and will be used against you in a court of law."

Dan spoke up weakly, "Hold on, let's not get carried away."

Dawn wailed. "I didn't attempt to murder anybody."

Sam continued, "You have the right to an attorney. If you can't afford an attorney, one will be appointed by the court to represent you. Do you understand your rights as I have explained them to you?"

"Sam, is this really necessary?" Dan asked.

"I'm afraid so. We don't know what's going on here, but the hospital found elevated traces of potassium chloride in your bloodwork. Someone tried to kill you last night, and until I have more facts, she will be in custody."

Dan said, "Dawn, don't say anything until you speak to an attorney."

Sheriff Sam directed the deputy to take Dawn to jail while Dr. Melendez joined the group gathered around Dan, which now consisted of Tripp, Anton and Candace. How Tripp ended up here, Candace didn't know, but she was glad he did. A discussion ensued regarding Dawn's proposed guilt and the likelihood of her innocence. They rehashed the evidence and timeframe. It was then the sheriff mistakenly mentioned the dogs had been poisoned.

The room filled with collective reactions. Sam looked contrite and the doctor immediately cleared out all visitors fearing the news might give her patient a setback. The doctor checked his vital signs and then left the room.

"Can I have a moment alone with my uncle?" Candace asked the men in the room. They quietly left, Tripp kissing her cheek and Anton retreating when he saw it. Once alone, Candace mustered up the courage to break the news about Merlin to Dan.

It was a blow, but not the first he had experienced in his life, and he seemed to take it well.

"What kind of monster would kill a dog?" he asked. "I doubt Dawn has it in her."

Candace kissed his cheek and held his hand. "I don't know what to say. "Uncle, I hate to bring this up now, but I spoke with Aunt Marj on my way here. She told me Uncle Eric threatened to kill Daddy years ago."

"That's what she told me. But I don't think he meant it literally. People sometimes say things."

Her voice cracked. "What if he did? Did the police ever investigate his threat?"

"Not that I know of sweetheart, but Eric is long gone so there isn't much use in stirring the pot now. After he shot himself, they were all gone."

"I guess." She shrugged.

"I'd like to be alone for a bit if you don't mind." Her Uncle looked bushed.

"Of course I don't mind. You've been through so much in the last few days and now, Merlin's death, I'm so sorry Uncle."

"Thank you. I just need to rest." He patted her hand and shut his eyes. She kissed him on a forehead deep with lines. Candace was so grateful he was alive, but someone had to find out who was trying to kill him.

Stepping into the corridor, an interesting troupe had assembled. The sheriff, Tripp and Anton were conferring with each other and the doctor.

"We've decided to move him," Tripp announced.

"Oh?"

"Yes, Ms. Kane," the sheriff spoke up. "He'll be safer that way. We'll get him a private nurse so his location can be kept confidential, and one of my men will guard him at all times. "No one will be allowed in without an ID."

"That's a relief, thank you," Candace responded. "If Dawn isn't the one who hurt him and didn't try to kill him last night, then who did?"

Tripp answered, "I still think it was the former girlfriend who, by the way, is staying at the nearby hotel where I am. Although I question the validity of her drug or poison knowledge."

"My money is still on your friend Dawn, but if her alibi checks out then I'm stumped. Everyone loves your uncle, and no one I have interviewed has a motive," said Sam. "Please think carefully. Is there anyone else who might want your uncle dead?"

"I just don't see how." Candace sighed. For the first time she didn't try to hide her frustration or exhaustion.

"I'm taking her back to the ranch to make her something decent to eat while you guys try to figure this out. I'm no real help here, and she looks like she's going to collapse." Anton put his arm around her shoulders even though she was standing next to Tripp, and she let him. Right now, she was desperate for some good food, a shower and some rest.

CHAPTER 32

It was dark outside when Candace opened her eyes. What time was it? She was on the couch in the family room, but the mess she had made with Tripp the night before was cleaned up, and quiet music was playing on the stereo.

Slowly, she began to remember the ride from the hospital with Anton earlier. They had a long talk about everything that had happened and called to check on their team. Not surprisingly Zach had the brunch set and everything was going well. Discussing the menu which started off with strawberries and whipped cream, prosciutto wrapped cantaloupe, spinach and artichoke stuffed mushrooms, and smoked salmon with bagels and cream cheese, made her even hungrier.

Cameron assured her their specialty vanilla bean ice cream French toast with bourbon syrup was already in the chafing dish, alongside the duo of western scrambled eggs, and paprika laced home fried potatoes. Although, she had tried to convince the bride to have eggs Florentine Benedict as well, they settled on the mushrooms.

Candace had added assorted tea sandwiches to the buffet to

blend the breakfast and luncheon combination, and it was much easier when wedding cake was the dessert. Both she and Anton genuinely cheered them on and were proud to hear all was under control. Of course, Candace would need to see pictures, talk to the client to make sure everything was up to their expectations and find out the amount of gratuity added to the bill.

After another hearty rendition of breakfast made by Anton, Candace was forced to take a shower and lie down on the couch. A change of clothes was sorely needed, and if she had to guess, it was now evening.

There was no sense wandering from room to room to find out who was home. She headed straight for the kitchen, Lancelot at her heels. Grand Central for the Kane family was always the kitchen, and Anton and Jesse looked at home sitting at the big table.

"Well, look who rose from the dead!" Jesse smiled.

It was so good to see her.

"Hi, how'd you sleep?" Anton chimed in. "We were just thinking about waking you. I talked to the doctor, and she said your uncle has been transferred to a private room and has a nurse at his bedside and a guard at the door. She thinks you should just let him rest and not try to come back tonight."

Candace looked at the clock. It was almost nine o'clock. "I guess she's right. I can't believe I slept so long."

"You needed it, Kalinda," said Jesse, ever the acting mom. "Now, we just need to bring your uncle Dan home safely."

"Did Tripp call?" Candace asked.

"Twice. I told him you were still sleeping." Anton's face showed no hint of how he felt about it.

"Wow, I must really have been out of it. Thank you, both of you for being so protective of me. I don't know how I would have gotten through this without your love and support, really," she said.

Anton snickered. "Don't worry, paybacks are a bitch."

It was then that she really felt in her heart they would soon be back to normal.

CHAPTER 33

A t 10 p.m. the hospital corridors were empty and sterile. A medium-sized facility in a small town, the patient count was low and so was the number of Sunday night staffers. Visitors were few, especially on the third floor, which was only for most dire cases. It was no wonder a woman could pass for any orderly or nurse, dressed in bright green scrubs with sneakers bound in funny matching baggies, wearing surgical gloves and make her way briskly toward the ICU.

Thank God the niece and her entourage were gone. If only he was gone too, the woman fumed. She had asked around, but no one seemed to suspect anything about last night's heart attack, and now she'd just have to give him more potassium and make sure he was dead. They said he was lucky last night because of all the machines attached to his heart. How stupid of her to have missed that. She would have to disconnect them just long enough tonight. No one should be able to tell what killed him.

Again, the guard was gone. Small town police departments were a bunch of clowns. They couldn't seem to keep anyone there with consistency. She was consistent. And persistent. They had no clue. She waited behind a column until the nurse's station was empty and the coast was clear. She'd only have a few minutes until someone returned to watch the monitors. Sliding the door back slowly and quietly, she could see his body lying there dimly lit.- That big hulk of a man whose very breath was destined to ruin her life.

She tiptoed toward the bed, needle in hand. Checking the IV for the correct port where the poison could be injected straight to his vein, she also found the power switch to the EKG machine.

Sticking the needle into the plastic connection, the woman pumped the contents of the syringe into the IV fluid. Her heart was beating with the count in her head. It should take about 1... 2...3 seconds to get into his bloodstream. She'd flick off the EKG, stop the tracking of his heart and wait. A buzzer should go off within a few more seconds, but she'd switch it back on, letting the nurses, generally a lazy bunch, chalk it up to a glitch in the print out or a mechanical error. In two or three minutes from now, she'd be in the clear, and Dan Kane would finally be dead.

It was deathly quiet. The clock on the wall ticked loudly enough so she could hear it. No sound came from the bed, but the EKG was still recording the rhythm of his heart. The entire dose was in his veins by now, but his heart was still beating. It should have worked by now.

"Hold it right there!" A voice boomed. The blinding overhead lights popped on. "You're under arrest."

"I...what? I was just checking on my patient," she said, cool as a cucumber, praying the EKG would not shut down now.

"Really? How am I?" Tripp sat up in the bed like a ghost wrapped in a sheet rising from the grave.

"You...I...what is this?" Her heart started to race.

"I'd like to ask you the same thing. Drop the needle and keep your hands where I can see them," Sheriff Sam demanded.

Tripp climbed out of the bed and stood beside her. "We've been waiting to meet you for several hours now."

"I don't know what you're talking about," she responded without hesitation.

Tripp said smugly, "Nerves of steel, I guess, Sheriff.".

"I guess so." Sam patted her down and picked up the needle. "Going purely by the description, I'm guessing this isn't the girlfriend."

"What's going on here? I was just checking on my patient, Mr. Kane. I don't know what's happening and why you're frisking me. This is ridiculous."

The sheriff demanded, pointing at her chest. "Oh yeah, where's your hospital badge?"

"I must have left it in the cafeteria when I had dinner. I'll go get it."

He let out a slow breath. "Sure you will. Listen lady, Mr. Kane hasn't been in this room since this afternoon, and if he was your patient, you'd know that. We knew the person who tried to kill him last night might return, so we set a trap for you. Thanks for obliging us and stepping right into it."

She dropped the façade and stiffened her back while she struggled against the handcuffs. "I want an attorney. This is entrapment."

"No, this is what you call good police work." Tripp nodded toward a smiling Sam.

The sheriff started leading her out of the room. "You might as well give us your name. I'll get it eventually."

"It's Pamela Lloyd Everett, and I demand an attorney." And that was all she would tell them.

CHAPTER 34

W hen the phone rang and vibrated like it had last night, Candace's blood ran cold. She could barely find the courage to answer it. She looked at Anton, then Jesse, then Anton again and handed him the phone.

He answered with his deep voice. "Hello, Candace Kane's line. Oh, hi, Tripp. It worked? Who was it?"

Candace stared at him completely puzzled.

"Hold on, she's right here." He handed her the phone back.

Candace said hello, and they watched her facial expression turn from fear, to confusion, then disbelief and shock. "That's Uncle Dan's former VP from his Denver office. She's the one? Damn."

Candace continued to listen and wasn't sure if she should wring all their necks for not letting her in on their plan or to just give them all hugs. Tripp explained that after she and Anton left to go back to the ranch, he and Sam formulated a plan to trap the would-be killer. They told Anton about it when she was sleeping, and the entire operation went down when she sat at home unaware.

She spoke with Sam and then Tripp again and hung up. That's

when her post nap, rested demeanor went into hyper drive. She let out a "Yippee!" that brought Lance to his feet. Hugging the dog, who was nose to nose with her while she was sitting down, Candace kissed him on the head and then jumped up to grab Anton.

Jesse was crying by the time Candace got to her. Anton grabbed a bottle of Vodka and poured a shot for each of them. It was definitely time to celebrate. They could all take a breath.

Candace was ready to clear the air and begin the healing process when Dawn's mother showed up the next day to facilitate her daughter's release. Marjorie made a statement to the police that incriminated her husband in a plot to kill Brad Kane. Candace sat by her side, horrified as her aunt remunerated what had happened. She told the sheriff that Eric, outraged over his wife's attraction to Brad, and deeply troubled about his poor financial standing, hired a man to stage an accident. When the deed was done, everyone assumed Eric was just bereft over the death of his friend, when in reality he could not live with the guilt. She swore he never would have planned to involve Cynthia or to leave Candace an orphan.

Killing himself must have been the result of his complete financial breakdown and blackmail. None of this became clear until after his death when Marjorie was approached by the actual killer. The "hit man" had tried to blackmail her as well, but once he found she would not fall prey to his threats, the man disappeared fifteen years ago.

She tried to find the courage to share the truth with Dan but just couldn't put him through yet another loss. After all, they were all dead.

CHAPTER 35

When the dust settled, Pamela took a plea bargain and not only admitted to trying to kill Dan in the hospital twice, but also confessed to aggravated assault for the attack at the ranch and the death of Merlin. Dan was adamant her sentence not be reduced any further for the sole reason she killed Merlin. He could not forgive the woman no matter what the extenuating circumstances.

At her preliminary hearing, she testified in court that because of the weight Dan carried in the securities world, she was unable to get even the lowest of positions in any brokerage house. Enough time had passed, financial market managers had changed hands, and a N.Y. office was willing to consider reinstatement of her credentials. However, the terms of her employment were that Dan would exonerate her from the fraud charges from seventeen years ago. She had emailed him, requesting in a letter he do just that and called him that Friday. He declined.

Convinced Dan would never give his blessing and would harbor lifelong resentment toward her because of the death of his friend, Eric Ehrlickson, she set out to remove Dan from standing between her and the career she had always excelled. All of her former actions, she contended, could be left to interpretation.

The day of the attack, she had walked in from the main road, and when greeted by the leaping and barking dogs, she enticed them with prepared chunks of Zoloft-laced sirloin steak and lured them behind the fence to the bunk houses. According to Pamela, she only intended to knock them out. She never intended to kill them.

When Dawn arrived just after she did, she spent the greater part of the afternoon hiding and hoping Dan would think Lancelot and Merlin had recognized Dawn and didn't react when her car pulled up. Her subsequent movements, closer to the house, were shielded by raised voices arguing about some old letters. It had been simple for her to sneak in behind Dan who was leaning against the mantel, seemingly dazed. Without disrupting him at all, she spied the fireplace tools, grabbed the poker and struck him firmly in the head. It was, as she stated, that simple.

The sun beating down on the gates of the Double K, created a shadow over the entrance as if outlining the path Dan should travel. Sheriff Sam led the mini-motorcade directly through them. Behind him, Tripp and his Dad drove Uncle Dan, followed by the mayor's car, flanked by two motorcycle deputies. Released from the hospital on Sunday, just two weeks from the day he arrived by ambulance, Dan looked much better than he did that fateful night, and Sheriff Sam told him so.

When they turned toward the house, Dan let out an audible gasp. "It looks like the entire town showed up for my return."

Lance greeted them at the front gate, jumping like a gazelle and barking up a storm. He ran alongside Sheriff Sam's car, played tag with the motorcycles from the highway entrance to the court-yard, then stood with paws on the edge of the fountain for a much-needed drink. Uncle didn't object, not today.

Sam had mentioned that he thought he might have to provide crowd control, but it seemed everyone knew to give Dan a wide berth, extending handshakes and hugs in moderation. The entire Double K staff and families were in attendance along with most of the usual annual BBQ attendees. Hospital staffers, nurses and physicians were invited, and Candace made sure Dr. Rachel Melendez was there. Friends and business associates came from all over the country just to celebrate Dan's survival and good health. Even Genevieve was invited but she declined to attend. Candace was sure it had to do with the updating of his will to exclude her.

To Dine For Catering catered the affair. Cheeseburgers of several combinations: bleu cheese and bacon, Swiss cheese and mushroom, which was Dan's favorite, and cheddar cheese with guacamole were served from one grill, while extra thick steaks made to order sizzled on another. A pig that Anton boasted was the size of a small horse was roasting front and center over a fire pit. To one side, were baked potatoes and a trendy hot corn station with seasonings and toppings like grated cheese, scallions and bacon bits to roll and coat the cobs.

On a buffet, covered in red and white checkered cloths, were gleaming white plates and white handled silverware. Wooden baskets overflowed with bread and rolls. Fresh fruit was displayed in carved watermelons in the shape of peacocks, turtles and whales. Bowls and chafing dishes filled to the brim with salads and side dishes, both hot and cold, led the way to a big black cauldron of Jesse's homemade chili served with beans and rice, done Mexican style, accompanied by ample chunks of jalapeno cornbread slathered in butter.

Cameron and Zach ran the show with the rest of the team present either as servers or guests. Candace stood beaming with pride. Those two young men possessed so much energy and focus and were learning things she had never been exposed to. Catering, in fact food service overall, was light years from where it had been when she was in school just a decade ago. The future of culinary creativity and where their business was headed was indisputable.

Tripp brought flowers for Candace–more than a dozen roses, each a different color. He said he wanted to find one as beautiful as she was but had to keep adding them since none of them compared.

Candace saw Anton roll his eyes and shuffle his feet in the dirt when he saw them presented. She just smiled and winked at him, knowing just what he was thinking because she had heard him say it before, "There was nothing worse than an American trying to out-romance a European man."

Though released from jail, Dawn was conspicuous by her absence. Anton was clearly relieved. Still Candace felt badly for her. Congressman Tethermeyer had discharged Dawn from any and all professional and personal commitments over the whole state of affairs, and her mother would barely communicate with her. I guess there really was such thing as Karma.

"I'm such a sap." Candace chastised herself as Jesse wrapped an arm around her waist as she gazed at the busy buffet. "I should be furious and never want to see Dawn again, but we have a history together and rewriting it is impossible. Besides, Uncle is safe and sound and business at To Dine For Catering is in better shape than ever."

Jesse looked at the Candace's old flame and gave her a squeeze. "This is true. You and Tripp seem to be closer than ever."

"We'll see." Candace gave Jesse a hug.

"Ah, Candacita, the past is the past, the future will be better. You will see!"

The End

ACKNOWLEDGMENTS

Immense gratitude to my BFF Judy Weiss, developmental editor, Kris Jordan of Skaowl Press, Natasha Brown and my personal coach, Ruth Goldberg Sharon, who collectively held my hand, cheered my efforts and by personal sacrifice of time and talent, helped make this publication a reality! To fellow authors and friends, Nancy Naigle, Jenna Blum, Sarah McCoy and Melissa Foster who made me believe this was possible, and to my family who had patience through the process.

ABOUT THE AUTHOR

Jerri George, a native Floridian with two grown sons and three grandchildren, is a thirty-five year veteran in event catering. Fifteen years ago, she relocated to her business and family to Denver, but at the height of her career, Jerri was sidelined by a near death bout of Bacterial Meningitis.

From her hospital bed, she not only survived but thrived by writing the best-selling, CIPA EVVY award winning book, *CATERSAVVY, Secrets of the Trade Revealed* in order to share her knowledge with others.

Having rediscovered a passion for writing, Jerri has focused on the creation of the *Candace Kane Chronicles*. Through *Murder on the Menu*, she shares the delicious and fast-paced world of catering well seasoned with a dash of romance and suspense.

https://www.amazon.com/Jerri-Lee-George/e/B00FRNAPDM

Made in the USA
Monee, IL
04 February 2021

59396094R00132